JULIAN

JULIAN

A novel

WILLIAM BELL

DOUBLEDAY CANADA

Doubleday Canada and colophon are registered trademarks of Random House of Canada Limited.

Library and Archives Canada Cataloguing in Publication

Bell, William, 1945-, author
Julian / William Bell.

Issued in print and electronic formats.
ISBN 978-0-385-68205-3 (bound) ISBN 978-0-385-68206-0 (epub)

I. Title.

PS8553.E4568J84 2014   jc813'.54   C2014-903131-9
C2014-903132-7

Jacket design: Leah Springate
Jacket image: © sparth/Getty Images

"Which Way Does the River Run?" lyrics copyright © Lennie Gallant (www.lenniegallant.com), used with permission.

Printed and bound in the USA

Published in Canada by Doubleday Canada,
a division of Random House of Canada Limited,
a Penguin Random House company
www.randomhouse.ca

10 9 8 7 6 5 4 3 2 1

For Jia Han

PART ONE

THERE MUST BE A RIVER

ONE

IT WAS ONE OF THOSE March days when all four seasons took turns playing hide-and-seek in the streets. Rain, sleet and snow rode across the city on blustery winds, and sunlight appeared only briefly through gaps in the roiling clouds.

A strange day, threatening or promising, Aidan couldn't decide. Maybe both, he thought, watching the buildings on University Avenue slide past the school bus window under a grey sky. Unpredictable? Definitely. He had awakened that morning with traces of an unfamiliar mood in a corner of his mind, like the residue of a dream. He couldn't shake the almost overwhelming feeling that something was going to happen, that his life was about to be altered.

By the time the bus drew up to the curb in front of the Ontario Art Gallery—joining a half-dozen others—the winds had calmed and a chilly drizzle had given way to snow. Around him, Aidan's grade ten classmates jumped from their seats, pulled backpacks from overhead racks and surged noisily toward the bus doors. Aidan waited until the tide of bodies had cleared, then stepped down from the bus, keeping apart from the boisterous throng on the sidewalk. Tall and fit, his team jacket tight across his shoulders, he could easily have passed for a young man four or five years older. He stood alone at the curb, still lost in the mood that had been with him since the day began.

He gazed across Dundas Street toward a row of old houses converted into boutiques and cafés, his attention seized by the falling snow. It seemed as if a hush had fallen over the city. As in a photograph or a painting, the space between the sky and the street was filled with white flakes that magically appeared out of the low clouds, thickened, then descended lazily through the still air to crumble and melt and disappear the moment they touched the ground.

A hand on his shoulder broke Aidan's concentration. A passing streetcar clanged its bell, rumbling along rails shiny with moisture. Cars and taxicabs hissed by. Snowmelt dripped from branches and overhead wires onto the pedestrians hustling along the sidewalk.

He turned to see his art teacher smiling up at him.

"Van Gogh awaits," she said. "It's not hockey, but you might find it interesting."

Ms. Sayers began to herd her students through the gallery doors into a lobby already packed with teens from other schools. Aidan hung back. A flash of colour had caught his eye—a sky-blue beret worn by a girl whose thick auburn hair was gathered at the back of her neck with a scrunchie. She was wearing a roomy camo jacket, cargo pants and military-style boots, and she was leaning against the gallery wall, her eyes on the crowd. Suddenly she slipped through the doors and blended with the mob.

Aidan followed. While he and his classmates checked their coats and backpacks, Sayers picked up their tickets at the reception desk and handed them around, reminding everyone to stay together and enter as a group. Strident young voices echoed as students massed before three harried ushers impatient to get into the exhibit.

Aidan saw the girl again. He watched as she insinuated herself deeper into the crowd. A few of his classmates began to horse around, bored by their slow progress. Someone lurched forward, falling against the back of the girl in front of him. She whipped around, red-faced, and shoved the already off-balance offender away. He collapsed into the mass. Raucous laughter. Jeers. People craned their necks, seeking the source of the disturbance. In the confusion, the blue beret moved quickly toward the exhibit entrance. Aidan watched the girl slip past the distracted ushers and disappear up the curved staircase.

Nice move, he thought.

In the first gallery given over to the Van Gogh exhibit, a large, dimly lit space with spotlit canvases ranged along the walls, Aidan sat on the long upholstered bench in the centre of the room and fished his assignment sheet from his inside pocket. Apart from drumming up enthusiasm in her class and lecturing briefly on the life and times of Van Gogh, Sayers had said little about specific works. She wanted her students to experience the paintings fresh, to see them as Van Gogh's contemporaries had, free of reputation and prejudgment. The task was a sort of treasure hunt. The students were to search out about a dozen paintings

Sayers had identified and note each one's place and date of composition. The second part of the assignment asked for personal impressions and thoughts on any paintings that stood out. "There are no right or wrong opinions," Aidan read from the sheet in his hand.

He reached down and massaged his ankle, still sore from last night's game. Aidan had slipped Daryl Findlay's check inside the blue line and swooped in for a shot on goal. Humiliated, Findlay had slashed him in retaliation, then sneered as he skated past him on his way to the penalty box.

Aidan got up and began a slow circuit of the crowded gallery, looking over shoulders and between heads for the works Sayers had identified. He made notes on each. Then he returned to the first of the paintings that had appealed to him. *The Langlois Bridge at Arles with Women Washing* depicted a horse-drawn cart on a stone bridge over a stream where a few women were cleaning laundry. As he began to write down his impressions, the blue beret bobbed into view among a clutch of middle-aged women and men with audio guides pressed to their ears. Together, they stopped before a canvas showing a sunlit field of flowers. The girl had opened her jacket and freed her hair. The thick auburn tresses brushed her shoulders, gleaming in the spotlights as she stepped closer to the canvas. Aidan consulted his notes. *Wheat Field, 1888.* The girl's beret was the exact colour of the sky above the field. She stepped back, melting into the preoccupied crowd, sidling closer to a grey-haired woman in a long leather coat. Aidan watched the girl dip her slender hand into the woman's tote bag, remove a purse and slip the prize into her own coat pocket. Nonchalantly she drifted to the next painting, paused for a few minutes, then sauntered into the next room.

Nice move again, Aidan thought. But he had read enough detective novels to know that the girl wasn't exactly a professional. The first thing a pickpocket wants to do is blend in. Her camo clothes and beret were like beacons.

Unsettled by the girl, he turned his attention to the papers in his hand. One of the questions asked him to identify his favourite paintings from the exhibit. Although there were more rooms of Van Goghs, Aidan decided to make it easier by writing about two he had already seen. *Wood Gatherers in the Snow* depicted a family trudging home at sunset along the edge of a canal or lake, dead tired under their bundles of sticks and probably looking forward to a soft seat and a cup of something warm. The painting caught the mood of a northern winter landscape already drained of light, the sky grey and cheerless and the snow dull. He liked the fact that Van Gogh had painted a family and that they were all together, but he didn't put that in his notes. *Boats on the Beach at Saintes-Maries de la Mer* couldn't have been more different. Four playfully coloured fishing boats rested on their keels under a Mediterranean sky bursting with light. The sails were furled, the gear packed away, the day's work done. Fishers and boats safe and sound at home—a feeling Aidan seldom experienced. He omitted that from his observations, too.

Sayers dropped down beside him on the seat.

"So, any thoughts? Which one are you writing about?"

"The one with the boats," he replied, not looking up from the page.

"Good choice. One of the more famous in this room. Any questions?"

"I don't think so."

"Alright, then."

Sayers rose and walked across the room to a quartet of students who seemed more interested in what was happening on the screen of a smartphone than the art surrounding them. Aidan finished his note and walked into the next room in the exhibit, hoping to see the girl-thief again. She was there, standing before a painting of a yellow house. Aidan approached slowly and stood beside her. She wasn't pretty in a movie star way, but there was something about her. The background murmur of people fell away. He could hear the girl's breathing, smell her skin. He wanted to feel her breath on his neck, to take her thick glossy hair into his hands.

Instead he pretended to be fascinated by the canvas. Children's colours, he thought. Buildings in strong shades of yellow, one with a pink awning, another with a red roof. A man walking past on the sidewalk. An impossibly blue sky.

"There's no way any sky could be that colour of blue," he whispered.

She turned to him. He had never seen such green eyes. She spoke with a trace of accent, her voice melancholy and soft.

"Oh, in Provence the sky is exactly like that," she said. "It's the bluest sky in the world."

"You've been there?"

"I was born there."

While people eddied around him, he cast about for something else to say, some clever words to keep the conversation going. But she turned away and drifted across the room to where a small group of women seemed mesmerized

by a night scene of swirling skies and exploding stars. Here
we go again, Aidan thought.

A uniformed guard was sitting in a chair by the door,
arms crossed over her chest, a two-way radio at her belt
leaking static. She was good at her job. Without seeming to
pay attention to anything in particular, she was watching
the girl.

Aidan crossed over, putting himself in the guard's line
of sight, and approached the girl from behind.

"The guard has her eye on you," he whispered.

The girl didn't react right away. She let a few seconds
pass, then, as light and unconcerned as a breeze, meandered
out of the gallery.

Behind him, Aidan heard boots on the gallery floor and
the creak of a leather belt. He waited a split second, spun
around and took a step, looking down at his notes, and
crashed into the guard, knocking her radio from her hand.
His papers spilled to the ground. He fell to his knees to gather
the sheets, getting in the guard's way as she tried to recover
her two-way.

"I'm sorry! My fault!" he said.

Her eyes were on the doorway as she tried to regain her
balance. "Never mind," she snapped, her face pink with
embarrassment. "Doesn't matter."

Aidan watched her go back to her seat, waiting for her to
use her radio. But she settled back and resumed her bored
expression.

Aidan was tempted to go after the girl. He tossed the idea
almost as soon as it crossed his mind. What would he say or
do if he managed to catch up with her? Mumble a few mean-
ingless sentences, probably. Make a fool of himself. He had

already crash-landed with his pathetic line about the sky in the picture of the houses. On the other hand, what did he have to lose? No, he should do what he was supposed to do—stay and complete the assignment.

He lowered himself onto the bench in the centre of the gallery, ignoring the patrons moving slowly from canvas to canvas, some speaking in hushed tones, as if in church. He took out his pen, tried to concentrate on the remaining questions, but the girl—her beautiful hair, her green eyes, her daring—pulled at him. He forced himself to resist. Eyes boring resentfully into the page in his hand, he skipped over the references to specific paintings and the invitations to share personal reactions of the "How does it make you feel?" variety to the final query, " 'Art is life.' Comment."

A typically vague, touchy-feely Sayers question. His eye travelled over the paintings opposite. A field at harvest time with a blue wagon in the middle. Another with irises in the foreground. Aidan wished art *was* life. If you didn't like the way yours turned out, you could do what a painter did—change it by painting over it. You could touch it up, make a few minor improvements. Or you could start from scratch and redo the whole thing, work away until you had something that satisfied you. It would be your painting, and you could do what you wanted. You'd be in control.

They said Van Gogh went crazy for a while and spent time in a monastery sanatorium or something. But they also said he did dozens of paintings while he was there— sometimes two or three a day. Wherever he was, each time he began a new work he started with a blank canvas. He decided the dimensions, the type of preparation, the subject. Everything. He took a piece of canvas and created what came out of his mind, anything from a plate of fruit to three fishing boats to a pair of old boots. If he made an error or changed his mind, his brush made what he didn't like disappear. Even a lousy painter controlled the project.

With a bitter, silent laugh, Aidan thought, if art is life, I'm not the painter; I'm the canvas.

Others made the decisions, set the goals, described his obligations. Others wielded the brush. It had always been like that. When he was younger, every time he had thought he was settled with a new foster family and could be normal for once, the ceiling fell in. His caseworker would speak to him, explain why he'd have to move again, assure him it wasn't his fault. Mr. Foster-McCallum lost his job and had to move out west for work. Aidan packed up his things and waited in the living room for a taxi. Mrs. Foster-Wainwright had been diagnosed with breast cancer and had a rough time ahead of her and couldn't handle an extra kid to care for. Aidan cleaned up his room for the last time, said goodbye and got into the back seat of his caseworker's car. And now it was beginning to look like life with the Foster-Boyds might also tumble down like a pile of pick-up sticks. He'd only been with them for about a year and a half.

He didn't blame the people at the Children's Aid Society. He didn't blame anyone. Sometimes he wished he could focus his anger and discontent on somebody. Instead, he stood quietly fuming on the sidelines while other people made decisions about every aspect of his life. Loneliness and instability had hardened him, and he looked at the world from behind a wall of his own making.

One CAS caseworker, Raleigh Diamond, got him into lacrosse. Aidan played for a couple of years, then quit when

Raleigh changed jobs and disappeared. Another, Jannie Sugarman, introduced him to hockey when he was ten. He liked hockey—most of the time—and turned out to be good at it, which pleased the Foster-Boyds, especially Henry. Aidan played centre and usually led the league in points. Now his life was a whirl of school, practices, games and sports camps. There had never been a minute of his time that was his.

The feeling that had almost knocked him to the pavement a while earlier as he stared into the hanging snow outside the art gallery swept over him again. A door was about to open, a curtain was about to be drawn. He was sure of it. Was it something to do with the girl in the blue beret?

Aidan jotted a quick note to Sayers on the blank side of his almost complete assignment and gave it to a girl in the class, asking her to wait a half-hour before giving it to Sayers. Then he made his way downstairs, collected his backpack and coat and pushed through the art gallery doors into the street.

TWO

AIDAN LOOKED UP AND DOWN the street but didn't see the girl anywhere. Disappointed, he walked into Chinatown and came to a busy avenue with streetcar tracks up the centre under a web of electrical wires. Snow continued to hang in the damp air, touching his face as he strode along, hands deep in his jacket pockets. Across the way a restaurant with a wide porch flanked by massive stone dragons dominated the corner, out of place in a neighbourhood of grocery stores, fruit stands spilling onto the sidewalk, and import-export shops peddling everything from cotton shoes to incense.

Delicious aromas wafted from noodle restaurants. Aidan's stomach growled. He peered at the menu taped to the steam-covered window of a small diner. He checked his wallet, shook his head and moved on.

He had had no plan in mind when he left the gallery.

His note to Sayers said only that he would find his own way back home. She'd be surprised. Aidan had never been a problem student, but he'd catch a load of trouble for breaking the school's field trip policy. He might get back home in time for supper, but it didn't matter as long as he made the game that evening. If he had to, he would go straight to the arena. Henry would bring Aidan's gear to the rink.

He headed north, then turned left where the avenue split to encircle a complex of old buildings. He turned corners randomly and soon realized he was lost. Good. Content to wander through the snow, he passed through an old neighbourhood of houses standing shoulder to shoulder with tiny shops.

After a while he found himself on a residential street flanked with maples, their branches black and wet against the sombre sky—a northern sky, not the brilliant blue upturned bowl of Van Gogh's paintings. He was enjoying the time on his own—a rare thing for him, free from schoolwork, practice, games. The boredom of swampy locker rooms, the mindless banter and pranks. The endless bus rides to and from arenas that all looked the same. Aidan usually passed the time reading. His teammates had harassed him at first and jeered at him, but they lost interest after a while. Over the years he'd burrowed through lots of detective stories—by Hammett, James Lee Burke, Chandler, Parker, Bruen and more. He liked detective tales because, at the end, things were put back together. Order was restored. A few months ago he had discovered a historical action series about Captain Alatriste, and he had put away two of the series already.

Thoughts of thrilling stories pulled the girl-thief to the front of his mind. It was one of the things about her that had attracted him as he watched her in the gallery earlier: she seemed adventurous. Fearless. Free.

It had stopped snowing. Aidan was alone on the quiet street. Up ahead he noticed a school, in front of it a break in the files of parked cars lining both sides of the road, leaving a safe pickup and drop-off area. A little kid emerged from the building, skipped down the steps and bustled along in Aidan's direction on the opposite side of the street. In addition to his backpack he was toting some kind of music case. A clarinet, maybe, or a flute. The kid was Asian, small, maybe in grade five or six, probably rushing to his music lesson.

Far behind the boy a compact SUV slipped out of the line of vehicles at the curb and drove slowly down the street. A cold, prickly sensation flowed up Aidan's spine and into his arms and hands. He stood watching the scene unfold. The dark vehicle drew to a stop about thirty metres behind the kid. Two young men scrambled out and began to shadow the boy. The SUV pulled forward, the image of overhead branches sliding across the hood and up the windshield, and drove past the boy. Abruptly it nosed into the curb, the hood dipping sharply as it jerked to a stop, and two more men jumped out, leaving the rear doors open.

Aidan realized immediately what was happening. It wasn't hockey, but the principles were the same. The kid was boxed by the four men. The two followers quickened their pace. But the kid had already caught on. In one motion he dropped the instrument case, shrugged off his backpack and dashed across the road. He cut between two cars and pelted down the sidewalk directly toward Aidan. Calling out to each other, the four men took up the chase.

Aidan felt a familiar jolt of adrenaline, his body's instinctive call to action. The kid flashed by. Aidan walked toward the men casually, as if he had no idea what was happening. One had already outstripped his partners and thundered toward Aidan, arms pumping, eyes focused on the boy. Aidan was suddenly glad he was taller and heavier than most teens his age. As the man brushed past, Aidan threw a hip check, launching the stranger over his back and into the street, where he crashed to the pavement, let out an explosive grunt and lay still.

Aidan steadied himself, then lined up on the second pursuer. The guy had seen what Aidan had done to his partner so he would be on guard. He'd probably try a head-fake. Training his eyes on his opponent's chest as the man barrelled toward him, Aidan took a step forward. The man feinted to the left but his shoulders tilted to the right, giving away his intention. Aidan dipped his knees, jammed his shoulder into the man's chest, heaved and, using the man's momentum against him, redirected his body off his feet and into the air. The man pivoted and tumbled with a crash into a row of trash cans, strewing garbage across the sidewalk.

Aidan snatched a glance over his shoulder in time to see the kid bolting between two houses, then turned back to the two remaining men quickly closing on him. They split up, like forwards rushing the net. As the first reached him, Aidan held up his hands, as if surrendering, and faked a smile, bringing a look of confusion to the pursuer's face. Still grinning, Aidan head-butted him. Aidan felt the blow in his forehead, heard the crack of bone, then a howl. Groaning, the man cupped his hands over his broken nose as blood dribbled off his chin.

Three down. By now the element of surprise had evaporated. Aidan scurried backwards to give himself room. The last attacker reached into his jacket as he rushed forward. Aidan heard a click, saw the blade, threw up his hands in desperation as the man lunged and slashed at his face. He felt a bee sting on his palm, then a burning pain. The attacker stumbled, thrown off-balance by his charge. Aidan stepped in and buried his fist in the man's stomach. As he grunted and folded, Aidan turned and ran.

He flew along the street and threw himself down the driveway where the kid had gone. Ahead, he saw the boy vaulting a fence. He must have watched the action from hiding before taking off when Aidan began his sprint. Trailing blood he hardly noticed, Aidan caught up to the boy on the road, loping toward a café on Dundas Street. Smart little guy, heading to a place with lots of people.

"Hold up!" Aidan called, pulling a hanky from his hip pocket and wrapping it around his hand. "They're gone."

The boy walked on without turning around. A few minutes later Aidan and he were sitting in a booth at the back of the crowded doughnut and coffee shop, the kid with his jacket over his knees to hide a wet spot Aidan had noticed but ignored.

"Who were those guys? Why were they after you?" he asked.

"You got a phone?"

"No, don't you?"

"It was in my backpack. I'm supposed to keep it in my pocket."

"Are you going to answer my question?"

The kid looked around, then got up, holding his jacket at his waist.

"Wait a minute," Aidan snapped. "Don't you realize you were almost kidnapped?"

"I'll use the pay phone," the boy said, and he walked away, picking his way among the tables to a phone near the washroom door.

Aidan followed. "You're not going to call the cops, are you?"

"No way."

While the kid used the phone, Aidan washed his bloody hand at the washroom sink, not quite believing that he had taken on four guys and left them on the ground. He was relieved that the boy wasn't going to involve the police, who would make life complicated for both of them. Dark red blood oozed steadily from the gash in the edge of his palm, opposite the thumb. He dried his hand as best he could, then rewrapped it in the bloody handkerchief.

The kid had been petrified by the ordeal, Aidan realized—so scared he'd wet his pants—but had shown no surprise. Most kids his age would have been babbling their heads off once they had their fear under control, wondering who the men had been and speculating as to why they had come after him. Not once had he suggested calling the cops or asking anyone for help. Aidan remembered thinking the kid had street smarts. As soon as the SUV had veered to the curb he realized he was in trouble, and he had known what to do.

Aidan found the boy standing beside the phone, his call completed. "You don't have to hang around," the kid said.

"Well, as long as everything is alright with *you*. What's your name, anyway?"

The boy replied by walking out of the restaurant. Aidan followed.

Outside it was cold, but the boy still held his coat at his waist, hiding the pee stain. Aidan knew the kid was probably acting like a jerk because he had been humiliated, hunted and terrified, chased through people's yards. With a high school guy right there, witnessing his shame. Aidan was familiar with the feeling.

"I said you don't have to wait with me," the kid repeated. "I can take care of myself."

At that moment a dark blue car swept into the parking lot and screeched to a stop. The back door flew open and an Asian in a dark topcoat got out. Aidan tensed and reached for the boy, but the man was holding the car door open and beckoning to the kid, who scrambled inside without a backward glance. The man slid in beside him. The car tore away as soon as the door closed, leaving Aidan alone in the snow.

Aidan made his way down to Queen Street and took the streetcar to the west end. As the vehicle trundled along the rails, he sat back and watched the crowded, rundown neighbourhoods scroll by the window. So much for an afternoon to himself. His escape from the art field trip to wander where his feet took him, to be alone for a while, had gone up in smoke, leaving only the weakness in his limbs from ebbing adrenaline. He had thought he had taken control, if only for an afternoon; then he had been blindsided by events set in motion by strangers, with nothing to show for it but a bleeding hand. He let out a bitter laugh. He had read somewhere that destiny didn't make house calls, that you had to go out and make your own fate. Whoever wrote that was full of it.

Or was he? Maybe destiny wasn't one thing or another. Maybe he was looking at the problem from the wrong angle. Yes, the attempted kidnapping had come out of the blue and Aidan had been caught up in it, but he had done something about it, hadn't he? Aidan reminded himself that he had saved the kid from being snatched—maybe killed. Maybe his thoughts when he was in the gallery mulling over Van Gogh and his art had been legitimate after all.

Be the painter, not the canvas, he had decided. He talked a good game, but could he follow through? How could he manage a change in his life? Waiting for someone or something to alter his direction meant he was the canvas, didn't it? He had to take some kind of action.

He had tried it once. A foster kid like him had two choices: he could rebel and run away, or try to go along, to be accepted. He had tried the first strategy back when he was taken in by the Foster-McCallums. Aidan had run off and won exactly four hours of freedom, then the cops had picked him up at the nearest mall and marched him to their cruiser under the noses of curious shoppers. He still remembered the sting of humiliation. After this short-lived rebellious period, when he realized that nothing of benefit ever had or would result from rushing into conflicts or win-lose dust-ups where a happy ending was not on the program, he had changed course.

Charging a brick wall with his head down hadn't helped, so he had tried to make his foster families like him. He had learned to go along, to agree, to harmonize, to please.

He held no resentment toward his fosters. He knew they got paid by CAS for letting him live with them, but he didn't think they did it for the money. They all tried to give him a home and make him part of their families. But he never was, never could be. He was a boarder. He now lived with Henry, Beryl and the twins, April and May. They were the Boyds. Aidan wasn't a Boyd. He was "... *and this is ...*" as in "Hello, I'm Henry. This is my wife, Beryl, these are my daughters *and this is* Aidan."

If he took off now, where would he go? How would he support himself? He was "in care" until he was of age—eighteen. He could get free sooner, when he was sixteen, if he wanted. But he'd still have the practical problems: nowhere to go, no way to earn money. Living on the street wasn't an option.

Until today, he had accepted that he was helpless, with no choices.

Sitting in the stuffy streetcar surrounded by strangers, peering though fogged windows at a blurry world, Aidan recognized that he had a lot to think about, a lot to figure out. But he knew that when you cleared away the deep thoughts and fine words, you came down to one basic truth: you're not what you say, you're what you do.

THREE

The nearer he came to the house where he had lived for almost two years, the more worry gnawed on Aidan's nerves. He had dreamed up a fictional explanation for the throbbing knife wound in his hand, but he planned to tell the truth about slipping away from the art field trip. As was his habit, he composed his facial expression, got his feelings under control, prepared to play the role he had adopted so often in his life. He became The Pleaser. He did not see this attitude as dishonest or hypocritical; he was not acting. Rather, he had trained himself to push down his anger, frustration and rejection—no matter how hard it was—and to sail toward smoother water.

Beryl's car stood alone in the driveway. Good. At least he could deal with the Foster-Boyds one at a time. He went into the house, shucked his backpack, hung his coat in the hall closet and ducked into the ground-floor bathroom. He unwound the blood-soaked hanky from his hand and dropped it into the toilet. He flushed, then held his hand under the faucet, working the dried blood from the skin. Wincing, he examined the wound closely for the first time. The blade had slit the thick edge of his palm, revealing red muscle beneath a layer of yellow fatty tissue. He searched the cabinet above the sink, finding a bottle of hydrogen peroxide and a box of Band-Aids. The h-p stung when he poured it onto the bloody gash, making a pink foam that dripped into the sink. He covered the wound with a couple of stick-on bandages.

Aidan headed for the kitchen, breathing in the aroma of beef stew. Beryl stood at the stove, a big wooden spoon in her hand. The twins, April and May, were busy at their homework, the table strewn with coloured pencils and books. The eight-year-olds had been born in the middle of the night on the last day of the month, April a few minutes before midnight, May a few minutes after. They took after their mother, inheriting her slight build and blue eyes and personality that sparkled like tinsel.

April looked up from colouring a zebra in green and pink stripes, a gleeful glint in her eye. "You're in for it," she said.

"Yeah, Mom's mad at you," May chimed in. "Aren't you, Mom?"

Aidan liked the girls; they were cute and funny, and most of the time they hid their resentment that they had to share their parents with him.

Beryl whacked the spoon on the edge of the pot and laid it on the stove-top. She turned and crossed her arms on her chest.

"Well, well, look what came in on the wind," she said, then demanded to know where Aidan had been, insisting on a detailed report, and why he had bailed out of the field trip, and did he realize the school had called her on her cell at work in the middle of giving poor Mrs. Quigley her bath, and did he have any idea how worried she had been?

"The art gallery was a colossal bore," he replied. "I decided to leave."

"And do what?"

"I just walked around. I kind of lost track of the time."

"That's not like you. Who were you with?"

"Nobody."

"Alone the whole time?"

"Totally."

Beryl's eyebrows rose skeptically; the corner of her mouth puckered slightly—an involuntary signal that she was weighing his statement. "You're going to catch trouble at school tomorrow."

"Yeah, you're in for it," April repeated.

"I can talk Sayers around," Aidan assured Beryl. "She's—"

"No you can't. Your absence counts as a skip. There'll be consequences. Detentions, probably."

May nodded wisely. "Consepences. Dimensions."

"Mom, he's got bandages on his hand," April accused, pointing.

"What happened?" Beryl asked, uncrossing her arms. "C'mere. Let me see it."

"I fell and landed on a piece of glass."

She cradled his hand in her own and peeled back the bandages, her professional manner taking over.

"May, honey, bring me my bag," she said, leading Aidan

to the table. She examined the wound. "It's clean but it's deep—and it'll need stitches." She looked into his eyes. "A broken glass wound, eh?"

Aidan remained silent as Beryl removed the materials from her bag and bandaged his hand properly.

"We'll have to have it seen to after supper. Henry should be home soon. You have a game tonight. I hope you'll be able to play."

"The playoffs," April said, her coloured pencil in motion.

"He's not going to be happy," Beryl said ominously.

"You're in for it," May added.

Beryl was right.

Henry had worked later than usual. He burst into the noisy dressing room, stuffing his gloves into his overcoat pockets, eyes scanning the room as he counted heads. He went to Aidan, shedding his coat and murmuring quiet replies to boys who tossed him a "Hi, Coach," as he passed.

"How's your hand? Can you play? What did the doctor say?" Henry snapped.

Aidan was awkwardly double-knotting his skate lace. "She told me I'd know for sure when the freezing wears off." He didn't add that strenuous activity might open the wound and delay healing.

Henry consulted his watch. "We've got lots of time. Hit the ice, see how it goes."

Aidan jammed his gloves under one arm, grabbed his stick and made for the door.

Henry called out, "You had to pick a playoff game day, didn't you?"

———

On the way home that night, Henry's displeasure with Aidan was eased by their win. The Mustangs had taken the game by one goal, scored late in the third period. Aidan had managed only two short shifts, his hand throbbing wickedly as he stickhandled. The team's place in the tournament final round was now assured, and they had two days off before the gold medal game.

If "off" was the right word. Henry had already laid out a practice schedule that filled every minute of the weekend—long distance runs through the streets, drills on the ice, analysis of plays—and had forbidden any social life for the players until after the final game.

No problem, Aidan thought. I don't have a social life.

Later that night, Aidan lay in bed, a dull ache pulsing in his bandaged hand. He thought about the upcoming playoffs and what they meant to him. He could still recall the early days of his career and the first time he had managed to stickhandle the puck from one end of the ice to the other without losing it. He was ten years old, and from that moment he was hooked. He was a latecomer but soon made up for it. He practiced hard, developed his skills, strength and timing. For him, nothing could match the thrill of a rush down the ice, the exhilaration of dodging an opposing forward and laying off a perfectly timed pass that whizzed up the ice and intersected the path of his teammate, ready to flip it into the net.

Aidan kept one secret to himself. When a play unfolded

like that, when the pass connected or when he himself shot the puck and the red light flashed, the goal was secondary. It was the perfection of the play, the rightness of it, that thrilled him, goal or no goal.

He was good—his record proved it. His teammates liked to play on his line because he passed more often than he shot, sometimes even when he had a clear shot on the net. His unselfishness made him popular on the team—even if they thought he was a little strange, with his long silences, his books, his reluctance to join in pranks and horseplay.

He kept himself apart for a reason. Making friends or becoming attached to his fosters had led to pain and grief when CAS moved him to another household. He had learned to insulate himself from loss. The ice was the only place where he allowed himself to dare, to take risks, knowing that, unlike his life, a hockey game was predictable. There were rules and patterns he could rely on.

Lately, or for the last year or so if he was honest, he had begun to tire of hockey and its demands on his life and attention. The game was a good friend, but one who never gave him time to do—or be—anything else. Even before the day at the gallery, when he had felt something shift inside him, his attitude to the game had changed.

As Henry had hoped and predicted—although Aidan's injury had shaken his confidence a little—the tournament trophy was carried off the ice and into the dressing room by the Mustangs' captain, Sebastian Vaughan. Aidan was pleased and excited for the guys on the team and for Henry, who had two loves in his life—his family and his team. Although Aidan's wound had kept him from playing his best—he had fumbled more than one pass that night—he had managed to score two points, both assists, and had shone at forechecking when the Mustangs had to kill penalties.

But the next evening at supper, Beryl was not herself. A light glowed in her eyes and she joked with Aidan and the twins even more than usual. Henry had called to tell Beryl that he'd be late for dinner and that they should go ahead without him. For once, Beryl didn't grumble and bang dishes around.

Something was up. Always sensitive to the threat that came with change, Aidan prepared himself for bad news.

FOUR

AIDAN LEFT SCHOOL the next day right after art class, his graded Van Gogh assignment stuffed into his backpack. Sayers had given him an A, then deducted a full grade for what she called, with a smile she'd been unable to hide, his "unauthorized exit" from the field trip. Aidan hadn't bothered to complain. He headed down Etobicoke Street toward home, pulling up his collar against the bitter wind that made the bare branches of the trees along the road click mournfully.

He remained ill at ease about Beryl's behaviour the night before. She had hinted once again about "big news." Why couldn't she just come out with it? He walked along, hating the uncertainty, chafing under the reminder that his life was still in the hands of other people.

He became aware of a car creeping along behind him, the purr of its engine barely audible above the huffing of the wind in his ears. The sedan kept pace with him. Aidan flashed back to the kidnap attempt a week before, involuntarily flexed his injured hand. He stopped, ready to dash back to the school.

The car came to a halt and a rear window slid down. A voice floated from the back seat. "Excuse me. Aidan Boyd?"

A man's voice, deep, calm. Neutral, the way you'd say, "Good day," to a stranger passing on the sidewalk. Aidan looked the car over. It was neutral too, neither shiny nor dirty; neither new-new nor old; the windows clean enough to reflect the clouds swirling in the sky. Keeping his distance, he bent and looked inside. It was the stranger in the dark topcoat who had picked up the boy outside the coffee shop, then sped off, leaving Aidan bleeding in the parking lot.

"May I speak with you?" the stranger asked politely, his words coloured by an English accent.

"Me? What about?"

"Please don't be alarmed. We met briefly not long ago."

"No we didn't."

"Well, no, not formally, I agree. I regret that the circumstances called for a rather abrupt departure. At any rate, I've been sent by someone who desires very much to meet you."

"Who? What about?"

He smiled. "You seem to have saved the life of someone my employer holds dear. I assure you, I'm no threat to you, despite this somewhat unorthodox meeting."

Aidan stood silently, his hands in his jacket pockets.

"Come along, please. I'll have you back here—or anywhere you choose—in no time."

The car door opened, allowing Aidan to see the man better. His black hair was combed straight back from a high forehead, his skin tight across his face. The hand resting on the car's window frame was uncallused, the skin smooth, the nails manicured.

"I didn't save anyone's life," Aidan countered.

"Wesley tells it differently, Mr. Boyd."

"That's not my name."

The man's eyebrows rose slightly. "I see. Then what should I call you?"

"Aidan."

"Very well. I am Mr. Chang."

Aidan's adrenaline ebbed as his alarm faded and curiosity took its place. What was this all about?

"How did you find me?" he stalled.

"Wesley remembered your jacket. It was quite easy to track you down. Although everyone seems to think your name is Boyd, probably because that is the name printed in block letters on the back of your hockey team coat."

"It's a long story."

"And an interesting one, I'm sure. I'd like to hear it sometime. But at present, here is the situation: I have been tasked to find you and bring you to my employer. I have completed half of my assignment. Should I fail at the second half, that worthy gentleman will be very upset with me. So . . . will you come? I think I can promise that you won't regret it."

Aidan recalled the stricken look on the kid's— Wesley's—face when he wet his jeans, his terror overshadowed by his humiliation. He had tried to bluff his way out of it by appearing tough and indifferent. Aidan had seen the relief in his eyes when the car roared into the parking lot—the same car idling at the curb now, a few metres away.

"Is Wesley okay?" he inquired.

"He's fine. And he regrets . . . well, I wish he could tell you himself. Please come. I mean you no harm," the tall man added, his voice as smooth as oil.

The smart thing to do was to refuse the request and go home. The whole situation was a little crazy. Why risk it? What was the point? On the other hand, maybe it was time for a change. Aidan approached and the man slid across the back seat. Aidan got in and pulled the door closed.

"Outstanding," Chang said, keying his cellphone and pressing it to his ear.

The car's interior smelled of leather and aftershave. Chang did not introduce the driver, who piloted the vehicle silently and smoothly, his square hands at ten and two on the steering wheel, his thick wrists at odds with the snow-white cuffs protruding from the dark blue sleeves of his suit. He drove south to the expressway, then along the lakeshore. After a while the car turned north and Aidan recognized the avenue where he had strolled along, free, after parting company with his school's field trip. He saw the intersection with the huge Happy Garden restaurant squatting on the corner, and was surprised when the silent driver made a left at the traffic light, then pulled into the restaurant's parking lot.

"If you'd be so kind as to come with me," Chang said as he got out of the car. "You may leave your bag in the car."

Aidan followed him through the side door of the building and down a wide corridor, its walls scraped and gouged—probably by the serving carts he saw standing idle in one of the rooms off the hall. He passed other rooms ringing with harried voices and the machine-gun clatter of knives on wooden chopping blocks.

He followed Chang up a carpeted staircase and along another corridor. At the end of the passage Chang stopped before a narrow elevator door and thumbed the keypad. They rode the elevator up a few floors, then the doors rolled open to reveal a spacious office panelled in dark wood, with a wide picture window. Three leather chairs had been arranged before a cold fireplace. Large fringed rugs covered most of the hardwood floor.

Chang removed his overcoat and draped it over the back of a chair. Unbuttoning his suit jacket he said, "Please take a seat."

Already second-guessing his decision to come, Aidan lowered himself into a chair, the leather creaking under his weight.

As if on cue, a large section of panelling swung into the room and a young man dressed in a black waiter's uniform entered, balancing a tray with a red clay teapot and three cups on it. He set the tray on a low table by the hearth and disappeared as silently as he had come. Chang sat down, adjusted his cuffs, consulted a thin gold wristwatch and settled back.

"When Mr. Bai arrives," he said, "don't offer to shake hands. And don't bow."

"Why would I *bow*?"

Chang didn't reply. Aidan looked around. What was he doing here? What did they want from him? His thoughts were interrupted by the click of a door latch. When Chang sprang to his feet Aidan rose too, as an elderly man appeared in the door frame. He was small in stature, more than a head shorter than Aidan, with snowy hair cut short and the bright eyes of a mouse—although there was nothing mouselike in the aura of authority that seemed to seep from him. Eyes on Aidan, he said something in Chinese.

"Mr. Bai has introduced himself, Aidan," Chang said, then broke into Chinese for a sentence or two, in which Aidan heard an approximation of "Boyd."

Bai gestured toward the chairs and they all sat down.

"Tell him my name isn't Boyd," Aidan said.

"From now on," Chang replied, "address yourself directly to Mr. Bai. I shall translate for both of you. Do not speak to me."

Bai had taken the chair opposite Aidan. He studied Aidan intently. Aidan did his best to hold the old man's gaze, noting the oval face with its strong features, the expensive fabric of the suit that rested easily on the narrow shoulders, the absence of jewellery, then the intelligent eyes again. He decided that "old man" was the wrong term for this guy. Bai looked over at Chang and nodded. Chang poured tea for the three of them, placing a cup before his employer.

Aidan was struck by the odd formality of it all. A tea party with two strangers in an office above a restaurant. In a voice both calm and reassuring, Bai began to speak again, accompanied by Chang's simultaneous rendition.

"I am very pleased to meet you, Mr. . . . . Aidan. Welcome to my office. It was kind of you to spare me some of your time. I hope I have not inconvenienced you too much."

"Why have I been brought here?" Aidan asked bluntly.

"Please forgive the unusual manner in which I have sought to meet you," Bai continued. "I see you are anxious to return to your own affairs. But if you would allow me a moment or two."

Bai spoke at length, with Chang providing the English. He thanked Aidan for saving his grandson, Wesley's, life, showed concern for Aidan's wounded hand and ended by saying that he was forever in Aidan's debt.

"I didn't do anything," Aidan protested. "Really. I just happened to be there. I reacted out of instinct."

"Your modesty becomes you" was the reply. "Wesley told me everything, in detail. And he asked me to convey to you his apologies for appearing both rude and ungrateful at the time."

I'll bet he did, Aidan thought, remembering the kid's attitude.

"And," Bai went on calmly, "we were able to . . . interview . . . the man who drove the car that day. We know everything, Mr. Aidan. You will have worked out that the four men attempted to kidnap my grandson, but their plans went wrong—thanks to you. Indeed, you probably saved Wesley's life. Now, Mr. Chang will explain," Bai said, nodding to his employee.

"Wesley was born in this city," Chang began, "but he is Chinese. His reaction when in danger is not to go to the police but to the head of his family, his grandfather. Wesley is Mr. Bai's only surviving male heir, and therefore more precious to him than his own life. He is now on his way to live in . . . Europe, where he will be safe. You must understand the enormity of Mr. Bai's debt to you, Aidan. He wants you to comprehend this. Fully."

"But—"

"You say you acted by instinct. And yet you stayed with Wesley. You had been knifed, but you didn't leave him to save yourself."

"What I'm trying to explain is, I didn't think about anything, like being in danger or . . . I just . . . did what I did."

"Nevertheless."

Aidan weighed Chang's words, but at the same time felt like a phony. He hadn't been overcome by a duty or desire to save the little kid he saw tearing down the street to get away from four men. He was an athlete; his body was trained to react without thought. Wasn't that what he had done? Alright, he had felt sorry for Wesley when it was all over. But how could he take credit for it, pretending he was a hero when he didn't believe he was?

Chang said no more. Bai crossed his legs, his fingertips caressing the chair arms. The silence weighed on Aidan.

"Okay, fine," he conceded. "Tell him I'm glad I could help, he doesn't owe me anything, and we'll let it go at that."

Chang rattled on in Chinese for a few moments. Bai nodded. Chang turned to Aidan. "Mr. Bai has given me permission to explain further. He has acknowledged his debt to you. Without your help his grandson might have been taken. Or worse. He cannot accept your answer. If you reject his gratitude he will be humiliated. He will lose face."

Aidan found himself at a loss. So unreal was the position he was in, he had no idea what to do or say. He only knew he didn't want anything from the old man sitting across from him.

"What should I say to him, then?" Aidan asked Chang. "I don't want to insult him. I already have, probably."

"No, not . . . yet. It's an old custom with Chinese of Mr. Bai's generation to refuse a gift two or three times before reluctantly accepting. And showing humility as you have done, saying you aren't worthy, is also polite."

"But I'm not being polite. I'm just . . . saying."

"I understand."

Aidan thought for a moment, then turned to Mr. Bai and said, "Thank you. I am glad to know I can rely on your help."

Bai seemed pleased. "Once again, I apologize for my grandson's bad manners. He is a naughty boy who has been spoiled and has always had his own way. He has much to learn."

"He was scared," Aidan replied.

"Your hand is healed somewhat?" Chang translated.

Aidan lifted his arm, flexed his fingers and wiggled them in answer.

"I am most pleased to know that," Mr. Bai said. "I hope you allow me to reimburse you for any medical costs you have incurred."

"You don't need to," Aidan said, "but, er, thanks just the same."

Then Bai stood, indicating that the interview was over. "Mr. Chang will provide you with certain information I would like you to have. He will be your liaison with me. Thank you again, Mr. Aidan."

After Chang had translated and Aidan had returned the goodbye, the old man left the room. Chang accompanied Aidan back to the car waiting by the door of the restaurant. On the return trip, no one spoke. When the driver turned into Aidan's neighbourhood Aidan asked him to pull over when they were still a few blocks from the Boyd house.

"I can walk from here," he said.

Chang looked as if he was about to object, so Aidan cut him off.

"The Boyds don't know about the, er, incident. They think I cut myself."

Chang nodded. "I see. Then let me take just a few more moments of your time."

He drew a business card from his pocket and handed it to Aidan. "My contact information, as Mr. Bai promised. You may call me any time, Aidan. I stress that—day or night, it doesn't matter. That number is a relay, as it were. Simply tell the person who answers the phone that you need me, then hang up and wait a few minutes. I am never out of touch. Never. Understood?"

Aidan nodded.

"It's imperative that you think about what Mr. Bai promised you and what it means. He was not simply being polite. He is a man of considerable resource and influence. There are many who would give everything they have to be under his protection."

"You make him sound like a godfather."

Aidan was pleased to see that Chang, for the first time since Aidan had met him, seemed puzzled.

"You know, like in a mafia movie," he added.

"Ah, I see. A joke. No, Aidan. You have a friend. Treasure that fact."

Not really, Aidan thought. Nobody made a promise like that without strings attached. In any case, it didn't matter. Once out of the car, he'd be through with Chang, Bai and the little jerk Wesley.

"Well, thanks for the ride," he said, opening the car door.

Aidan got out, but before shutting the door he said, "You never told me who tried to grab Wesley."

"Let us call them business rivals and let it go at that," Chang replied in his smooth, superior way.

Aidan flared, felt the heat rise into his face. The tension of the meeting broke through.

"I get it. You tell me I saved Wesley's life, make promises, and when I ask you a simple question you give me the brush-off."

Chang thought for a moment before answering. "Very well, Aidan. Mr. Bai's business dealings are extensive, but you'll never see or hear his name on the news. He guards his privacy jealously. One of his projects is a very large real estate development—I won't bore you with details—and his acquisition of this extremely valuable parcel of land created a certain amount of envy among rivals who had also bid on the land, and lost. This organization then attempted to purchase the land from Mr. Bai. Of course, he refused. Hence the kidnap attempt. Wesley was to be a sort of bargaining chip."

"Okay," Aidan said. "I get it."

Chang offered his cold smile. "Goodbye for now."

Aidan turned and walked up the street toward the house where he lived.

FIVE

AIDAN SAT AT THE SMALL pressboard desk in his room at the top of the attic stairs, looking out the dormer window at a sky streaked with cloud, thinking about the months to come. A week-long holiday from practices and games— then hockey camp. Why it was called camp was a mystery. To Aidan the word suggested a lake with tents along the shore, bonfires at night and canoe or sailing lessons under a hot sun during the day—not an arena echoing with shouts and whistles and the scrape of skate blades on ice, and humid dressing rooms smelling of socks and liniment.

He allowed himself to daydream of a real camping trip. It was easy to do, since he had no experience to contradict his fantasies. He imagined day after day of unplanned time, every hour filled with nothing but possibility. But his reverie was broken by the ring of a phone downstairs, followed by a torrent of words from Beryl. Aidan got up and closed the bedroom door, trying without success not to think about the topic of Beryl's excited conversation. In mid-August the Boyds—plus Aidan the boarder, if he wished—would be moving to Calgary. For good.

He didn't wish.

On the day after Aidan's interview with Mr. Bai, Beryl and Henry finally broke the news that Beryl had been holding in for the last while. Henry had come home from work on time for once, and when the family sat down to supper he explained in a voice as calm as Beryl's was bubbly that he had accepted an offer to run his own real estate franchise in Calgary, Alberta.

"He'll have six agents working under him!" Beryl crowed.

The twins were swept along in the current of their parents' excitement.

"What's a calgry?" April asked, her eyes bright with borrowed enthusiasm.

"Calgary, honey," Henry replied. "It's a big city out west with parks and movie theatres and—"

"—and a river that flows right through the middle of it," Beryl chimed in.

"And a famous hockey team," Henry added, with a glance at Aidan.

"Can I be on that team?" May asked.

Aidan had thought he was prepared, but when he heard the news his stomach dropped and a sick, empty feeling crept over him. He swallowed and tried to stifle his feelings. He began to work out what Henry's decision for his family meant for him.

Would the Boyds really want him to move to Calgary with them? Or was Beryl, who Aidan knew was kind-hearted underneath all her noise, just trying to let him down easy? If he didn't go west, he would be absorbed back into The System until his caseworker found another family who would take him in. Teenage boys, he knew, were hard to place.

Did Aidan want to move? In Calgary, almost 3,000 kilometres away, he'd be absorbed into a different province's system, with a new caseworker.

Either option meant a new school, a new hockey team, new pals—if he made the effort to meet friends, something he hadn't really managed in the last few years. What was the point, when he might have to say goodbye to those friends if everything was yanked out from under him as it had been before?

There was a third choice, but it was fantasy. It would be about two years before he could walk away from The System and be on his own, with nobody telling him where to go and what to do when he got there. Was that freedom, when he *had* nowhere to go? No job? No place to live? Panhandling on the streets and sleeping in a box had no appeal either.

Aidan got up from his desk and fell onto his bed, hollowed out by fear and loneliness.

When Aidan was in grade six and living with the Foster-McCallums in Woodbridge, Linda would sometimes let him stay up late and watch TV with her. He liked Linda. She never showed him anything but kindness. She was a chubby blonde who wore a lot of makeup and clothes that were usually too tight. Aidan was old enough to know that Fred, her husband, liked her that way.

Fred worked rotating shifts and sometimes didn't get home until ten-thirty or so, and Linda felt a little lonely in the evenings. One night she tuned in an old movie Aidan had never heard of. The main character, Huckleberry, was a boy about Aidan's age. A sort of foster child who lived with the Widow Douglas in a little town in Missouri on the Mississippi River in the 1800s, Huck had grown up wild. Widow Douglas did her best to civilize him, making him go to school and do chores and wear unfamiliar, itchy clothes, and sit still when company came. One day when Huck couldn't stand the strict discipline anymore he lit out with a neighbour's slave. The two of them escaped down the Mississippi on a raft.

As if the similarities between Huck's situation and Aidan's weren't enough to keep him interested in the movie, he was hooked by the idea of leaving all his cares behind and drifting away on a broad, beautiful river that seemed to go on forever. What could be better?

From then on, Aidan loved rivers. Any time a school project was assigned he asked to do a report on one. To him, rivers were fascinating, more mysterious than the sea, more exciting than the call of a distant train. A river always changed, yet stayed the same. It began at your feet and could take you to another place and, Aidan thought, maybe another life.

Whenever things got bad for him he would tell himself, somewhere there must be a river.

The next morning gusts of icy wind flung fistfuls of rain from a dirty sky. Aidan left the house at the usual time, the hood of his raincoat cinched tightly, his backpack thumping between his shoulders like a nagging pain, his mood as foul as the weather. During his first class, English, he was barely conscious of Mr. Topp's lecture on writing the short story. He stared at the streaks of rain on the classroom window, following one after another as it took its zigzag course to the sill.

". . . the so-called third-person narrative," Topp droned, "gives us a tale told by someone other than the main character—the protagonist. Take, for example, *For Whom the Bell Tolls*. Robert Jordan is the protagonist, but not the narrator. You recall Robert Jordan, do you not, Aidan?"

Aidan's mind snapped into focus. "Yes, sir. Spanish Civil War. He, er, dies at the end?"

Topp barely acknowledged the reply before marching on. "In third-person storytelling we have a number of advantages which I will explore later. On the other hand, to use Aidan here—who appears barely able to stay awake for this lesson—as an example, we have the first-person narrative."

Aidan flushed as scattered laughter erupted around the room. He began to pay attention.

"If Aidan says, 'I this and I that,' 'I thought such-and-such' or 'I ran toward my future,' he is telling his own story," Topp continued. "In first person, as we say. The first-person narrator speaks directly to the reader. He tells a tale about himself. Think of Holden Caulfield in *Catcher in the Rye*. The narrator may omit facts or include them, exaggerate or not, give us half-truths or the whole truth, all according to his own personality. The main point here, young ladies and gentlemen, is that the first-person narrator may tell us what he wishes, in the way he wishes. After all, it is, as I said, *his* story."

For a split second Aidan felt dizzy. His fingers gripped the edge of his desk, his thoughts whirling. Telling your story. Painting your picture. The metaphor was different, but the meaning was the same.

He glanced toward the window, where rain continued to stream down the glass. The time had come. He knew it. What he had been waiting for since the day at the art gallery and the girl with the blue beret and the falling but not falling snow—what he had almost come to believe would never happen—had burst into view, riding on the words of his English teacher like foam on the crest of a wave: "He tells his own story."

The moment the bell sounded to end the lesson, Aidan was on the move. To his locker, out of the school, down the street through the pounding rain to a convenience store where he knew he could find a pay phone. He pushed through the door, dropped his backpack on the floor, pulled out his wallet, removed a business card, jammed coins into the slot, punched in the number printed on the card.

After one ring, a neutral voice: "State your name."

"Aidan."

"You're calling from where?"

Aidan told him.

"Number?"

Aidan read out the digits printed above the phone's keypad.

"Hang up and wait."

There was a click. Aidan replaced the receiver and stood staring out the store window, the rain-lashed glass blurring his view of the street outside, the air in the shop hot and damp. He felt enclosed, cocooned. His jaw muscles clenched. The phone rang.

"Hello."

"Aidan, how pleasant to hear from you." Chang was as smooth as ever. "How can I help?"

"You told me Mr. Bai would give me anything I wanted."

"He would indeed."

"Can he make me disappear?"

PART TWO

LIFE IN THE FIRST PERSON

It was kind of solemn, drifting down the big, still river,
laying on our backs looking up at the stars. . . .

—Mark Twain, *Huckleberry Finn*

S I X

And so "Aidan" dropped off the face of the earth, like a speck of dust.

How could I give up my name? Easy. The way I pictured it, a person was like the solid disc at the centre of a target, encircled by concentric rings. The nearest and strongest ring was made up of parents, brothers and sisters. The next one was grandparents; then aunts, uncles, cousins and so on—all bonded by blood and branded by name.

But I had no family. I knew nothing about anyone who might be related to me. Take away the rings and what was left? Just me.

Put another way, "Aidan" was like one of those labels attached to a package with a bit of wire. Tossing away a used tag and twisting on a new one was simple.

I never knew why I'd been called Aidan in the first place, or who chose the label, and I didn't care. For all I knew the name hadn't been given to me by a birth parent at all. It could have been selected at random by a delivery room nurse or a social worker who ran his finger down a list and didn't get past the As.

"Julian Paladin," my new handle, was a fresh beginning. It made me feel a little different; it gave me another chance, like a hundred January firsts rolled into one.

My new identity came on a day at the end of April when Chang visited the apartment where I had been living since I disappeared a month or so before, and laid a small stack of documents on my kitchen table. He had been thorough. There were school records; a birth certificate that indicated Vancouver as my birthplace; a driver's license showing I was now eighteen years old; a social insurance card (I'd need it for my new job); a health insurance card—everything, even a passport. I had two credit cards in my name. It was identity theft in reverse.

"Just a few things," Chang said, "and I shall be on my way. Please listen carefully. You are a polite young man and you'll naturally want to contact Mr. Bai and thank him for his assistance. Don't. If you must communicate with him, go through me as I instructed you previously. That is his wish." He placed an embossed business card on the table. "George Wang is a lawyer who serves Mr. Bai. Should you require legal assistance of any kind, get in touch with him. He has been briefed to respond immediately and to assist you in any way he can. He will charge you no fee."

Chang closed the catch on his soft leather briefcase and began to button his coat. When he spoke again, his smooth, neutral tone toughened. "Finally, three most important points. If anyone—*anyone*—should ask you about Mr. Bai, you do not know him or anything about him. Indeed, you have never heard of him. That is absolute. If you wish to show him your gratitude, this is how you do it. Secondly, remember that you are to ignore the comings and goings in the two spare rooms downstairs. Thirdly, do not attempt to contact either me or"—he tapped the business card with a manicured fingernail—"this gentleman by means of the telephone in this apartment. Use a pay phone until I can provide you with a secure cell. I trust I make myself clear."

I nodded, my mind racing, wondering if I had somehow landed in a spy movie.

After Chang left the apartment I heard his footsteps on the stairs. The sound of the front door closing sent a ripple of anxiety across my brain. I was free; I was alone; I had gotten just what I asked for. I felt like I was sitting on a makeshift raft of logs, floating down a broad river as an unfamiliar landscape slipped by on either side of me. It was exhilarating, and for just a split second it scared the hell out of me.

My apartment was one of three in an east-end house built a long time before I was born. A Scottish woman named Fiona lived in the attic apartment above me with her preschool son. An older man lived on the ground floor and gave mandolin lessons once in a while. His place was on the left when you came in the front door to a hall that extended through to the door into the garage. On the right of the entry, a staircase with a newel post and wooden bannister climbed to the second floor, occupied by my apartment, and further up to Fiona's place. Behind the staircase, invisible from the entry door, were two doors leading to separate single rooms.

The house sat on a big corner lot in a residential neighbourhood of mature trees that canopied the streets. The landscaped front yard was enclosed by a low wooden fence with a gate, and guarded by an ancient oak whose roots buckled the sidewalk that bisected the lawn. The house, with its full-width verandah, was the kind of place you might see in an old movie—not at all like the newer suburb far on the western edge of the city where I had lived with the Foster-Boyds.

Mr. Bai had insisted, Chang told me, that I didn't need to pay rent. I had argued that I did. The whole point of changing my identity was to be independent, and that meant free of obligations, at least as much as possible. But paying rent meant I needed a job, and it wasn't long before Chang solved that problem for me too, finding me a part-time spot in a nearby convenience store. I worked mornings. Also, I became a sort of unofficial caretaker of the house. I collected the rents, mowed the lawn, trimmed the hedges, and I had a number to call if anything in the way of house maintenance was needed. I knew my rent was very low, but at least I wasn't a parasite.

I couldn't leave the Foster-Boyds in the lurch, wondering what had happened to me. I didn't blame them for deciding to move to Calgary. At least, I tried not to. It was a great chance for them, with Henry's new position and the opportunities it opened up for the family. The twins were young enough to get used to a different school and new friends, and they were thrilled by the idea of a bigger house and yard and Henry's promise to put in a duck pond. I admit I was put out for a while when they made their decision final and told me about it over the kitchen table, explaining that I could come along, that I'd be just as welcome as now. They meant well, but I wasn't part of the excitement that thrummed like background music in the house. I didn't expect to be. They didn't owe me anything. It wasn't as if I was hoping or expecting that they'd adopt me. Their decision was one more push in the direction I wanted to take anyway.

On the morning I shoved my raft away from the river bank I wrote them a note. Told them I was cutting out for good. Said not to worry, I'd be alright and I'd drop them a line now and then to prove it. Assured them the move to Calgary was not the reason I was leaving. I thanked them for being good to me and included a goodbye to the twins. I couldn't think of anything to add.

I propped the note on the desk and picked up my backpack. I had stowed my few important belongings in it the night before. I stood in the bedroom doorway and took a look around the room. Down in the kitchen, April and May were chattering away while Beryl tried to hurry them up to get ready for school. I tried to count the number of bedrooms I'd stayed in over my life—the one- or-two-night perches and the places where I was there long enough to fill a dresser drawer or two and hang my shirts in the closet. Rooms in social services facilities with cheap furniture and the smell of cleaning fluids, with bedsheet corners pulled as tight as drumheads; rooms in chain hotels; rooms in real houses where I allowed myself to hope it'd be a long stay this time, and did my best to adapt to the new fosters.

This time, I told myself, it was I who was making the change. I went downstairs, said goodbye as I did every morning, headed down the street toward my school.

And kept right on going.

SEVEN

THE ISTANBUL QUICKMART was ten minutes' walk from the house. It was run by a middle-aged man named Gulun Altan and his wife, whose first name I never learned. I figured Bai owned the store, or had a stake in it, or at least something that gave Chang the leverage to get me in. Gulun scowled at me when I showed up at 7:45 the first morning but thawed out a little as he showed me my duties—which included stocking the shelves, sweeping the floor, taking out the garbage to the alley behind the building. I did my best that first day and every day after, and I could tell that both he and Mrs. Altan respected hard work.

Gulun was dark, short, pot-bellied, bug-eyed and as bald as a lacrosse ball. Every day, he wore a white long-sleeved shirt and necktie. Mrs. Altan was also short—and round—and favoured dark shapeless dresses under a smock. The Altans spoke in an accent he told me was Turkish, and both he and his wife put in long hours, sharing shifts and keeping an eye on the anti-theft mirrors hung in the ceiling corners opposite the counter. They lived in an apartment above the store.

I wasn't allowed behind the counter, where the cash register sat beside a flat glass case full of lottery tickets. Besides the usual wide range of stuff—from milk and dry goods to newspapers and magazines to greeting cards and a thousand different kinds of sugar drinks—the Altans sold illegal cigarettes and pirated DVD movies under the counter.

A lot of the customers were regulars, picking up necessities or magazines, or a coffee from the self-serve machine beside the pop cooler. One of them was a guy who had some kind of storefront office a few doors down the street. He came in at the same time each morning for a coffee and the newspapers, always wearing either a dark blue suit or a dark grey suit with a clip-on tie, and the same black leather shoes. He had a thin moustache and a goatee.

One morning he called me over from filling the potato chip rack and told me we were out of coffee creamer. I went out back and returned with a carton of powdered creamer sachets and placed it beside the coffee machine.

"You don't work here afternoons," he stated, stirring the white powder into his cup with a plastic stick.

"Just mornings."

"Mmmm."

Unsure whether the comment applied to the coffee he had just sipped or my answer, I said nothing.

"And you look like a guy who can take care of himself."

I shrugged.

"Think you might be interested in a little extra work?" he asked.

"I don't know. Doing what?"

He shot a glance toward Gulun at the cash register.

"This and that," he replied. "Odd jobs. Sometimes I could do with an extra pair of legs, you know, when I'm tied to my desk at the office."

"What kind of office?"

"You're very direct. I like that. And I can tell you've got a head on your shoulders. I practice law."

Somehow, with his scuffed shoes and clip-on tie, he didn't fit the image of the attorney with a dozen suits in his closet and a Mercedes parked at the curb.

"And you want me to—what?—run errands, stuff like that?"

He nodded. "Something like that. What do you say?"

He was being vague. And he was flattering me. Why not come out with what he had in mind?

"I'll think about it," I said.

"I pay cash. Strictly off the books," he added with a knowing look. "Minimum wage. Name's Curtis, by the way. And you're Julian, right?"

I nodded. He gave me a smile that didn't show in his eyes. "Drop in today when you're finished here. I think we'll work well together," he said, and headed to the front to pay for his coffee and papers.

Some adults think people my age can be easily pushed around. A few encouraging remarks, a couple of compliments—they figure that's all it takes to get their way. Curtis seemed to be like that. But that was okay with me. Let him think what he wanted to think. Playing hockey and lacrosse, not to mention a lifetime in social services, had taught me that it's a big advantage sometimes when people underestimate you.

When I finished up at the store I hung my apron on a peg behind the door to the back room, said goodbye to Mrs. Altan, who didn't look up from the order sheet she was filling out, and walked down the street to a little Italian café. I asked for a wedge of pizza and carton of milk at the counter and took my lunch to a table at the back. The pizza was lousy and usually barely lukewarm, but it was cheap. As I ate, I thought about my encounter with Curtis. Was it possible that CAS had tracked me down, that he was working for them? The thought made my stomach drop. Unlikely, I reassured myself. Very unlikely. I was being paranoid. But it wasn't hard for someone like me—on the run, with too many secrets—to be suspicious of just about anyone.

I knew the cops would have been alerted that I had hit the streets. The Foster-Boyds would have contacted CAS as soon as they read my letter, and they would have informed the police and filed a Missing Person report. But the cops had a long list of runaways; everybody knew that. They couldn't hunt for all of them. And CAS—according to my latest caseworker, who complained about it every time I saw her—was always understaffed. They had enough problems on their hands. Sure, they'd put out the word, ask around, but that and registering me with the police was about all they could do. Besides, I was living far across the city from the Boyds' place.

I relaxed a bit. I wasn't interested in working for Curtis, but I figured I'd meet with him just to rule out the chance that he was onto me. If I decided he wasn't, I'd see what he had in mind. The more I thought about it, the more I reminded myself I could do with the extra money.

A group came through the café door and took a table. A family, it looked like—two adults with a boy and a girl. The girl sat down sideways in her chair, head lowered, her back to her mother, her face half screened by long sand-coloured hair. Making a statement. The boy, around eight or nine, a couple of years younger than the girl, plunked his elbows on the table and gave all his attention to the video game device in his hands.

The dad conferred with the woman, then went to the order window. Mom reached into the pocket of her torn yellow windbreaker and peeled the wrapper off a stick of gum and handed it to the boy. Without taking his eyes off his toy, he stuck the gum in his mouth, folding it double on his tongue before he chewed, and continued with his game, rhythmically thunking the heel of his running shoe against the leg of his chair. The woman gazed vacantly at the far wall, turning a pack of cigarettes end for end, over and over, as if the motion had hypnotized her. Her pale round face looked tired and careworn. The girl worked hard at ignoring her surroundings.

The father slouched over to the table, carrying a tray of food and drinks. He distributed slabs of pizza on paper plates, then set down four cans of pop, each with a straw sticking through the zip tab hole. None of them smiled. Nobody spoke, not even to persuade the girl to eat her pizza before it got cold.

You'd never see this foursome pictured on a billboard in one of those happy-loving-family scenes created to make you feel warm and fuzzy about the product being advertised. They were just ordinary people, not too well off if their clothing was any indication.

And I would have bet the kids, each in their own way, didn't realize how lucky they were. They took their parents for granted, knowing, without even thinking about it, that their parents would look after them. Their parents would be there in the morning when they got out of bed knuckling the sleep from their eyes. Every day.

I gulped down the rest of my milk, folded up the pizza wrapper and stuffed it into the bin on my way to the door. As I passed the family's table the father said something to the girl. Her head snapped up. She tried not to, but she laughed. Then all of them started eating.

Curtis's office was jammed between a Vietnamese manicure salon and a small engine repair shop that had a couple of old gas-powered mowers on display out front. It had once been a store—I could tell from the display shelf in the front window. A sign above the door read "A.T. Curtis & Associates." I found him at his desk, his jacket hung on the back of the chair, his shirt sleeves rolled up, typing away on a laptop. A cracked plastic radio on the shelf behind him was playing middle-of-the-road music just loud enough to be irritating. The office was rundown-looking, with chipped furniture and bare floors. There was nothing on the walls but a calendar showing the wrong month under a picture of a sailboat—no framed licenses or degrees, which may have answered my doubts about Curtis being a lawyer. He hadn't said he was, not strictly speaking. He had said he practiced law.

Curtis looked up when he heard the door close.

"Ah, good. Glad you could make it," he greeted me, closing the lid of the computer. Then, gesturing, "Take a seat."

I dragged a wooden chair over to the desk and sat down. Curtis started in right away.

"Know how to use a cellphone camera?"

"I guess I could figure it out if I thought about it long enough."

He ignored my sarcasm and rummaged in his desk, coming up with a cell. He powered it up and held it so, if I leaned forward, I could see the keypad and screen. "Push this button to bring up the camera function, and this one"—there was an electronic click—"to take the picture. Simple, see? Just be sure whatever you're taking is in the centre of the screen so the camera knows what to focus on. Think you can do that?"

I felt my jaw tighten. "I guess."

"Here, try it."

He handed me the cell. I took a photo of the radio and showed him the image on the screen, then put the cell on the desktop.

"Okay," he said, picking it up. "Now, you push this button to call up the photo library and this one to scroll through the pics. You can practice later. Take a few shots, then erase the pics like this."

The photo of the radio disappeared. He pushed the phone across the desk toward me. I left it there.

"So you want me to take pictures for you. Of what?"

He sat back and, with his thumb and index finger, smoothed his moustache and goatee.

"Not what. Who. I'd like you to follow a certain person, unobserved of course. Anyone she meets, anywhere she goes, take a picture. For people I want the face, for places the address—a photo that will identify the place. Digital pictures are always time- and date-stamped, so you don't need to write anything down. With me so far?"

I'm not a moron, I wanted to say, but instead I nodded.

"If she gets in a car, photograph the license plate. If it's a taxi don't bother. If that happens or if you lose her, call me. Use the cell; it's a prepaid unit. No need to use your own."

No problem there. I didn't have a cell. Chang hadn't come across with the one he'd promised, and I figured he wouldn't want me to use it for this stuff anyway.

"Who is it you want me to follow, and why?"

"The who is just someone we'll call the subject. The why is nothing for you to worry about. I can't divulge that. It's privileged info."

I must have looked doubtful.

"Don't worry; I'll make it worth your while. Keep track of your hours and any expenses—transit tickets, whatever—and you'll be reimbursed. If this works out, there'll be more work for you."

"The same kind of work? Following people?"

"That, and other things. Look, why not give it a try? You have nothing to lose, right? Do this one job, then if it's not for you we let it go. No harm, no foul. What do you say?"

"How do I find and recognize the, er, subject?"

"So you're in?"

I nodded.

He slipped a photo from one of the file folders on his desk and handed it over. It showed a well-dressed woman about Curtis's age emerging from a revolving door in an office building, looking toward something in the street. The brass sheathing around the door frame indicated that it was an upscale place. The woman carried a briefcase in her hand and a purse hung from the opposite shoulder. She was pretty, with fair hair and an open face.

"She leaves this address," the lawyer informed me, jotting some words on a sticky-note and pressing it onto the back of the picture, "every day at one o'clock. Give her until one-thirty, and if she doesn't show, break it off and call me."

I stood up, slipping the photo and note into my shirt pocket. "I'll give it a try," I said.

"Good man. Start tomorrow. Continue every weekday afternoon until further notice."

I was almost out the door when he called, "And Julian? This is just between you and me, right? Client confidentiality and all that."

EIGHT

AFTER MY VISIT to Curtis's office I went home. I liked coming back to my own place—turning the key and climbing the stairs and letting myself into the silent apartment, where everything was as it had been when I left. If I had forgotten to turn out the light or close a kitchen cupboard door, I had no one to answer to but myself. The book I was reading lay on the table beside the chair by the window, my laptop—used, supplied by Chang—stood closed on the desk beside the bookshelves I had made of bricks and boards. From the kitchen, the refrigerator motor hummed quietly.

Sure, once in a while I sort of missed the twins tearing through the Foster-Boyd house and yelling for their lives, or the savoury aromas of Beryl's cooking as she banged around the kitchen. I was never not lonely, but I was used to it.

Following habits learned early during my stays in foster homes, I kept the place tidy. Being neat and orderly had been a way to get fosters to accept me right away—every parent likes a tidy kid, and I discovered that a lot of people think neat equals good. I had made my bed every morning, folded my clothes and put them away in dresser drawers, kept my hair combed, lined up my cutlery in the proper manner beside my plate before I began to eat. Nowadays none of that was required, but old habits die hard.

I pulled on my running gear and left my apartment. I jogged over to Coxwell and turned south and followed it down to the lake, where I picked up the bike path and headed west toward Harbourfront. It was a sunny afternoon, with a light breeze off the lake. Once on the bike path and free of pedestrians and traffic I put on a little speed, cruising along at a comfortable pace while I analyzed my meeting with Curtis. There was something about him I didn't like, but I couldn't put my finger on it. I tried not to let that influence my thinking. I knew that following a woman and recording her movements on behalf of a lawyer was just a sneaky form of information gathering. A divorce case, maybe. Or was Curtis working for an insurance company? Was the woman scamming the insurers, pretending to be injured and disabled and collecting payments? Maybe she had been in a car crash and claimed to have whiplash or something.

She didn't look like a scammer, with her businesslike appearance and good looks, but that didn't mean anything.

Nor did I have an answer to an even more obvious question—why me? If Curtis was collecting info on the woman for a client, why not use a real private detective?

The only answer I could come up with was that he was paying me minimum wage—in other words, getting me cheap. But why would he care about that? Wouldn't he just charge the cost to the client? Unless he was doing just that: billing for a real detective, paying me—what? a fraction of the cost?—and pocketing the difference.

Or was there a client? Was this case personal? Was the woman his wife or a girlfriend who was two-timing him? If that was true I was being paid to stalk the woman—a pretty revolting thought. On the other hand, if I didn't do it, he'd just get someone else. That was no excuse, though. If it turned out he was using me to stalk her I'd sign off.

And another question. Why the photos? I could easily and less conspicuously follow her and make notes on her movements and meetings. Therefore, he needed pics to be able to prove where she had been, at what time and with who—without involving me. He'd just hand over the photos to the client. Which, to my relief, probably cancelled the possibility that this was a personal thing.

As I passed Harbourfront, where the bike path ran parallel to the pedestrian sidewalk, I slowed to dodge tourists and shoppers. Could I follow someone without being seen by her? I had read enough detective and cop novels to feel pretty confident that I could pull it off. Unless she was alerted to the possibility that she was under surveillance and was looking for a tail, she'd have no idea. I had read lots of cases where the main character followed from behind, from across the street, even from in front of the subject. In one book the cop doing surveillance by following the bad guys in a car would take three or four hats with him and change headgear every little while. A subject checking his rear-view mirror would see a different guy each time. I could do that. I could blend in. No problem.

I had to admit that I was a bit excited by the plan. Who knew, maybe it would be interesting.

The next morning was busy at the store. Deliveries from suppliers seemed to arrive at the alley door all at once, and soon piles of cartons filled up the back room. Gulun was in a bad mood and demanded I deal with all the new stock right away. It was slow work because I had to be sure I shelved the new stuff behind the old and turned the packages and cans so that the expiry dates weren't visible. Gulun always insisted on that.

As soon as I shook free of the store I rode the subway to Union Station and walked up Bay Street and located the address Curtis had given me. It was an office block with the name of an insurance company over the door. I loitered in the doorway of a pub across the busy street, checking my watch every few minutes to make it look like I was waiting for someone. It was a sunny day—not that you'd notice easily; the soaring banks and office buildings blocked all but a thin rectangle of sky—and pedestrians schooled up and down the sidewalks like shoals of fish. Mostly suits and well-dressed women. On a nearby corner a bunch of bicycle couriers lounged around, their bikes within reach, tossing wisecracks back and forth.

At one o'clock sharp, just as Curtis had said, the woman emerged from the building. She was wearing a blue suit and her hair bounced on her shoulders as she strode down the street and turned at the first corner, heading west. I tailed her, keeping in mind the tips I had picked up from books, like making sure that I was at least twenty or thirty metres back and that there was at least one person between me and her at all times. She kept up a brisk pace, her hand clamped on her shoulder bag, her body swaying easily as she walked, like an athlete or someone who made regular visits to the gym. At St. Andrew station she took the steps down to the subway.

I boarded the car behind hers and took up a position by the door. At the Dundas Street station she got off, took the stairs to the surface and strolled west, more slowly now, turning north on McCaul, striding along in the shade of the trees. She turned into a boutique restaurant—some kind of upscale Middle Eastern place, with a menu displayed in a glass-fronted box on a post outside. I walked past, realizing right away I couldn't follow her in. The place was so small there would be no dark corner where I could sit and observe her secretly. Besides, I probably couldn't afford even a glass of water in there. So I jaywalked across the street and stood beside a flower stall, in the shadows, leaning against the alley wall. I took out the cell and snapped a picture of the restaurant.

She had entered the place alone. If she was meeting a friend, they'd probably leave together. I could get a shot of the two of them. All I had to do was wait. So I pulled a paperback from my pocket and tried to read, glancing across the road every few minutes. Captain Alatriste was chasing the Pirates of the Levant—which was a funny coincidence, because the restaurant was called Foods of the Levant. The book told an old-fashioned story, part of a series that took place mostly in Spain a long time ago, with lots of adventure and sword fights and beautiful women and tough, brave men who would draw a sword or dagger in a flash to defend their honour, or the honour of one of the beautiful women. As I read I was conscious of people passing, drifting into the edge of my vision, momentarily blocking my view of the restaurant, then slipping out of sight. It happened dozens of times. Then someone stopped. I paid no attention. Until I heard a voice I recognized.

"Well, well. A literary loiterer."

She stood there blocking my sightline to the restaurant, hands on her hips, the sun behind her. She had rolled up her camo jacket and tied it around her waist. The military pants and boots were the same—and so was the blue beret, worn at a rakish angle. But it wasn't her clothing that made everything around her seem to disappear.

At the Van Gogh exhibit I had glimpsed her eyes only briefly, and in dim lighting. Now she stood—in my way— drenched in early afternoon sunlight that set her thick auburn hair blazing, highlighting her amazing green eyes. She was about shoulder-height on me, slender, with a faint spray of freckles under her eyes and a mischievous look on her face.

I closed my book self-consciously and jammed it into my pocket.

"Remember me?" she smirked.

"Sort of."

Which was an understatement. I had thought more than once about her, the mysterious thief with the French accent who had sneaked into the gallery and stolen at least one wallet from unwitting women before she disappeared.

She had been the brightest part of a day that was—to say the least—eventful.

I took a step sideways to keep the restaurant door in sight.

"A month ago, wasn't it?" she asked.

"More like two. It snowed."

"Not in the gallery."

I forced a laugh at the lame joke. How could I get her to stay? I rummaged around in my brain for conversational ploys.

"I was on a field trip," I explained. "Art. Well, obviously." I felt the blush rising into my face.

Her look was full of challenge. Come on, it seemed to say, impress me. Give me a reason not to move on. Or was I misjudging her? After all, it was she who had stopped to talk. She could have breezed right on by and, intent on my book and my stakeout, I wouldn't have noticed. I made myself try again.

"Anyway," I began.

"I owe you one," she interrupted.

"Er—"

"For warning me. At the gallery. About the guard watching me."

"Oh, yeah. Right."

"So how about I buy you a coffee or something?"

"Sure. Yeah, good," I stumbled. "I'd like that. You can tell me more about the sky in Provence."

She smiled again. The girl who had asked a few minutes ago if I remembered her. How could I forget?

"Well, let's go. I know a place near here."

Just then the subject came through the door of the

restaurant. With a man, who held his hand in the small of her back, as if guiding her to the street. They turned south, walking side by side.

Dammit. Now what to do? Break off the trail and go with the girl? I could tell Curtis the subject hadn't shown at one o'clock, that I'd hung around for a half-hour, as he instructed me. But he'd demand to know why I hadn't called him. Or I could say I had lost her—and he'd never hire an incompetent like me again. While I wavered, the man and woman continued along, moving farther and farther away. In a few minutes I really would lose them.

"You coming?" the girl asked.

"Er, I just need to make a quick call first."

I took out the cell, pretended to key in a number. "It's me," I said to the silent phone. "Now? Can't it wait? Alright, yeah."

I shoved the phone back into my pocket.

"Sorry, I gotta go. Maybe—"

Her face clouded. Her eyes hardened. "I get it. Some other time."

"I mean it," I blurted. "I want to."

But she had already begun to walk away.

"Where can I find you?" I called out.

"The park behind the art gallery," she replied over her shoulder. "Sometimes." And she turned up a side street and was gone.

Cursing my luck, I dashed across the street and hurried to catch up to the woman and her friend—or lover, or colleague, or brother, or whatever he was. In the distance I caught sight of them as they turned onto Dundas Street in the direction of University Avenue. Once they were out of sight I ran to catch up, slowing as I turned the corner. They were ambling along, as if stretching out their time together. At the subway entrance, they stopped. And kissed.

Mystery solved. Not a brother or colleague. I had time to get three pictures. It was a long kiss.

I tailed her back to the office, snapped one last shot as she pushed through the office building door, then called Curtis. He said to come straight back. I logged my time and expenses into a small notebook I had bought at the QuickMart that morning. On my way to Curtis's office I detoured to the park where the girl said I might find her. She wasn't there.

Curtis was happy with my work when I recounted the woman's lunch date and showed him the pictures. He hooked the cell up to a little printer and ran off a couple of copies of each photo. After examining them, especially the kiss, he beamed. His grin confirmed that the assignment hadn't been personal; it was for a client.

"Great work," he said. "I have all I need. You won't need to follow her again."

"Okay."

"So, if I need you for another job, are you up for it?"

"I guess so."

"Good. Now, I have a lot of work to do, so if there's nothing else . . ."

I fished out my notebook. "Yeah, there is. You owe me for two and a half hours and two subway tokens."

NINE

THAT EVENING, I climbed the narrow stairs to the attic apartment. On the way up I whispered, "Julian," to myself a few times. That morning Gulun had called me to the cash register and for a minute or so I kept stacking the shelves by the coffee machine and didn't answer. I had thought my new name was second nature by then. I'd have to be careful.

I knocked softly on the door. From within I could hear a television, a baby crying, a woman's soothing voice. It was my first go-round on rent collection, part of my job as caretaker of the house—not a hard task, I thought, since there were only three tenants and one of them was me.

Fiona yanked open the door and stood red-faced and flustered, her toddler balanced on one hip, a steaming mug on the table behind her. A large plaque on the wall read, I'M NOT THE GREATEST MOM IN THE WORLD BUT I'M TRYING.

"Oh!" Fiona said. "Julian. Um, come in."

Despite the open window over the sink the cramped two-room apartment smelled of fried sausages and dirty diapers. There were recently used dishes on the kitchen table and the high-chair tray was smeared with blobs of dark green something-or-other. Fiona lowered the baby into a mesh-sided playpen in front of the TV, used the remote to switch from news to a cartoon channel, then shoved a clothes rack draped with baby clothes against the wall, out of the baby's reach.

"Come and sit down," she invited, gathering the dishes and piling them in the sink. "We were just finishing supper and I haven't had my well-earned break yet. Your timing is perfect. Cuppa tea?"

I took a chair. "I guess so. Thanks."

Fiona was a small woman—in height—plump, with jet-black hair worn short and straight. A florid complexion and a button nose over a small mouth gave her a no-nonsense expression. She filled a mug with tea the colour of chocolate, topped up her own and shoved the milk jug and sugar bowl across the table to me.

"Settled in alright, are you?" she asked. When she spoke she rolled her Rs and cut off her Ts.

"Yeah, pretty much."

"Grand. It's a bonny place to live, this house. Quiet neighbourhood, decent landlord, and enough heat in the bloody winter, not like my old place. And between you and me, the rent is fair."

The baby was standing in the playpen, gripping the frame in both hands and shaking it as if attempting to tear it apart, giving out a stream of gurgles and chirps.

"What's his—her—name?" I asked.

"Roger. He's two. My wee man, but a handful, I can tell you."

"He seems to like the cartoons."

"Aye. I hate to plop him in front of the tube like that, but it gives me a bit of a breather."

Both of us stared at Roger for a moment, then I said, "Um, I'm supposed to collect your rent. Is that okay?"

"Aye, I guessed as much. Won't be a tick."

She bustled into the other room and came back with an envelope, which she placed in front of me. She sat down and took a sip of tea.

"So, Julian, are you working these days?"

I told her about the convenience store, but not Curtis.

"Going to school?" she asked. "University? College?"

"No. I'm done with school, for now anyway." And glad of it, I thought.

She raised her eyebrows expectantly, inviting more information, but I said nothing. She smiled.

"Alright. Understood. Enough said. A man who keeps his counsel, I see. I'm a nurse at East General, up Coxwell there. And as you've probably noticed from my comings and goings, I work shifts. I've only been there a few years, so my seniority is low and I get pushed about on the roster at times. Roger's daycare is with a woman down the street. God, I was lucky to find her. She's a treasure."

"Well, I guess I better—"

"Oh, stop awhile and have another cup of tea," she cut in, jumping up and filling the kettle before I could put in a word. She chatted on about her job, the doctors and patients and other nurses, and I came to the conclusion she was lonely. Maybe the job and the kid filled her life. One look at the apartment told me a nurse didn't make much money. I knew she didn't have a car. After she wound down a bit I made another try.

"Well, thanks for the tea," I said, picking up the envelope with her rent in it. "I better get going."

"Not at all, Julian. Drop in any time."

The contrast between Fiona's little apartment and the one on the main floor couldn't have been more dramatic. Thad Rawlins insisted I call him "Just Rawlins—everybody does" as he shook my hand at his front door. He invited me into a spacious room flooded with evening light from the two bay windows, a room that looked like a cross between a bookshop and a music store. A keyboard flanked by tall loudspeakers stood by one window, an open laptop and other electronic components I couldn't identify lined up along the headboard above the keys. By the other window an array of instruments—two guitars, a banjo and a mandolin—stood in their stands like benched athletes ready to be sent into the game. Stacks of books and magazines and sheet music hid the top of a wide coffee table in front of a leather couch. And every inch of available wall space was covered with full bookshelves.

Dressed in denims and a long-sleeved collarless shirt under a leather vest, Rawlins himself was tall and lanky and loose-boned. Everything about him—his face, his limbs, his fingers—was long. His voice was deep and scratchy and resonant.

"Come on in," he insisted when I told him my mission. "Take a load off. I'll go get the tribute."

I didn't know what tribute meant but I didn't say so.

I lowered myself onto the couch. Rawlins came back into the room, his slippers brushing the threadbare rug, a wad of cash in his hand.

"Good thing you caught me today," he said. "Had a gig last night and I haven't had a chance to blow all my coin on used books or fast women."

I jammed the money into the envelope Fiona had given me.

"Sorry about the small bills," he said, smiling. His teeth were long, too. "That's what happens when you get paid out of the bar receipts."

"That's okay," I said.

Rawlins sat down and crossed his ankles. "So, how do you like it here?" he inquired.

"It's okay."

A chuckle rumbled. "You're pretty easy to please, Julian."

"No, really. I like it."

"Little Roger's bawling doesn't get on your nerves and keep you awake?"

"I can hardly hear him. It's not a problem."

I didn't add that I liked the muted sounds that came from upstairs: the baby fussing at night, Fiona's footsteps overhead, her voice as she soothed her baby.

"Nice girl, Fiona."

"Yeah, I think so too."

"Ever hear people out there in the downstairs hall? Or the spare rooms?"

"Not so far, and if I do I'm not supposed to talk about it."

"Falls into the Mind Your Own Business category, right?"

I nodded.

"What about my music students murdering Appalachian ballads on the mandolin or guitar?" he continued. "The only thing worse than a baby screaming is someone missing the frets."

"Doesn't bother me," I replied truthfully.

"You like the mandolin?"

"I guess so. Well, not really, if I'm honest. It's a bit plinky-plunky for me."

This time Rawlins laughed outright. "'Plinky-plunky!' I'll have to remember that. Sure you don't mean the uku-lele?"

"I don't think I've ever heard one."

Rawlins leapt to his feet, fetched the mandolin from its stand, rummaged around in a vest pocket and came up with a pick, and took his seat. He whipped the instrument's strap over his head.

"This is sort of like a uke," he explained, playing a snatch of a tune I didn't recognize, making the mandolin sound, well, plinky-plunky. "Sound familiar?" he asked.

"Sort of."

"That's a badly played mandolin. I shouldn't say 'badly.' My students are learning the fundamentals. Here's what it should sound like."

This time the sound was full and rich on the deep notes, clear and ringing on higher notes.

"Okay," I said. "Definitely not plinky-plunky."

Rawlins chuckled again, returning the instrument to its stand. "Kinda music do you like?" he asked. "Rock? Alternative? Folk?"

"I don't know anything about music. I hardly ever listen to it."

"I think you may be the first person your age I've ever met who didn't listen to music. You don't even have a favourite band?"

I shook my head.

"Well, you and me are going to have a lot to talk about next time you visit. And if you ever want a lesson . . ." He let the thought hang.

"Yeah, er, maybe. I'll think about it."

Smiling, he replied, "Try to harness your enthusiasm."

"Okay," I said, getting up and moving toward the door.

"See you, Julian," he said.

TEN

THE NEXT DAY I planned to deliver the rent money to the address Chang had given me, thinking I might as well drop it off during my daily run; it would give me a destination to head for. At home in my kitchen after work I spread a city map across the table and used the index to find the street I wanted. It connected to Spadina, near Mr. Bai's office above the restaurant with the dragons.

I had learned nothing new about the old man, but Chang had told me he was a property owner. I assumed Mr. Bai owned the restaurant and the house where I lived and the store where Mr. and Mrs. Altan presided over the potato chips and pirated DVDs.

I gave my attention to the approximate route I would take across the city, making sure to include the park behind the art gallery, which the map told me was called Grange Park. I pored over the grid of streets as if reading a book. I preferred paper maps to online versions. My fascination with rivers, and all the projects I had researched, had led me to a love of maps too. I liked the idea that I was looking at a piece of the world in two dimensions. I'd study a map, with its mountain ranges, cities, coastlines, and I'd imagine what it was like to live there.

The city I was looking at now had a few sizeable streams—the Humber, Don, Rouge and, farther out, the Etobicoke and Credit. What was it like back in time, I wondered, before there was a city here? One thing was for sure—those rivers were different now.

I changed into shorts and a tank top, slipped the rent money into the small, teardrop-shaped backpack I used for running, and left the apartment.

The sky was overcast, the air hot and clammy and still. Thunderstorm weather. But I decided to go anyway. My hopes rose with every step I took toward Grange Park. Would she be there? Would she be angry at me for what she must have thought was a brush-off on McCaul St. that day? I slowed as I came down Beverley, passed the gallery and jogged into the park. The threatening sky hadn't scared off many people. A pickup soccer game was underway on the grass. Most of the benches were occupied by street people grabbing a nap, or men and women reading books and drinking from paper cups, or kids just hanging out.

But I didn't see the girl with the blue beret.

Disappointed, I turned and jogged toward Spadina and found the street I was seeking. It wasn't much more than an alley. A sign hanging out over the narrow pavement advertising the Chongqing Gardens promised "Real Szechuan Cuisine." The restaurant window was strung with red paper lanterns hanging over a bank of garish colour photos showing plates of food that looked like plastic.

Inside, the place was more like a long hall than a restaurant, with a counter inside the door where a grey-haired woman wearing a cardigan and a toque perched on a stool behind the cash register, reading a Chinese-language newspaper. Mrs. Zhu, I guessed, the person who would receive the rent money from me every month.

She looked up when I approached, eyed me up and down, the forehead above her plate-shaped face creased by a frown, her wide mouth turned down at the corners.

"You wan' eat here or take out?" she demanded. "Maybe takeout is best."

"Mrs. Zhu?"

She nodded. The frown disappeared, the mouth formed a smile. "You Julian."

I nodded, unzipping my pack. When she saw the envelope she shook her head. "No, no. Not here. Sit in back. I come in a minute." Then she screeched something in Chinese toward the rear of the restaurant.

None of the customers—all men, all hunched over their bowls of rice or noodles—looked up as I made my way to the one empty table in the shadows at the back. As soon as I sat down a young woman, her hair jammed under a paper hat, her brow beaded with sweat, crashed through the swinging kitchen doors, plunked a bowl of steaming liquid in front of me and disappeared as quickly as she had come. Savoury, spicy steam clouded from the bowl.

A few minutes later, Mrs. Zhu shuffled to the table and took a chair. "Eat," she commanded, pointing at the soup.

I was hungry from running, still too heated to eat, but

I picked up the porcelain spoon. The spicy liquid seemed to explode in my mouth, a brew of unfamiliar flavours laced with fire. I coughed and spluttered, but the trickle I managed to swallow was delicious.

"Hah!" the triumphant Mrs. Zhu proclaimed. "Not used to good food."

"I think I'll just wait till it cools a little," I wheezed.

"Now you give money."

I handed over the envelope and zipped up my pack. Mrs. Zhu counted through the bills, then stuffed the envelope into her pocket as if it was a used tissue. From the other pocket she took a cellphone.

"From Chang. It safe. You eat here any time. Not pay. Eat good Chinese food. Westerners no good at cooking. Ruin everything. Now I go back."

And with that she made her way to her stool and newspaper. I tried the soup again, sipping carefully from the spoon. It had cooled, but the peppery, blowtorch intensity of the spices hadn't. I finished it, then got up and left. Mrs. Zhu didn't look up as I passed her, but when I pulled the door open I heard her parting words behind my back.

"You be careful, Julian. Many shark in water."

Wondering what she meant, I walked through the darkened alley to Spadina, then began to jog toward Grange Park. It was on my route home. Sort of.

The girl was there.

The sky had darkened and the air seemed even heavier and more oppressive. The soccer game had folded up and gone. A few of the teenagers hanging out on the benches looked at the clouds apprehensively. The girl was sitting alone at a stone table under a shade tree, writing in a notebook.

I walked up to her, suddenly self-conscious in my running shorts and sweaty tank top. My heart was leaping in my chest and my mouth had gone dry. She didn't notice me; she kept on writing—or printing. Rows and columns of numbers flowed from her pen.

She was wearing a baggy white T-shirt, faded and threadbare. She had pulled her hair back from her face, giving her a slightly severe look. She had a wide, pretty mouth with an ironic twist in one corner.

"Well, well," I said, "a numerate note-taker."

It was the closest I could get to her calling me a literary loiterer a couple of days ago, and I thought I was being clever. As soon as the words passed over my teeth, I regretted them.

But when she looked up and saw me she smiled. "You found me," she said, slapping the notebook closed and capping her pen. "Come to collect your debt?"

A gust of cool wind swept across the park grounds, stirring up dust and bits of paper, just as thunder boomed above the city. She stuffed her belongings into her satchel and scrambled to her feet.

"No, I just wanted to see you."

"Let's get out of here," she said.

We ran across Dundas to a coffee shop and stepped inside just as a blast of rain peppered the window. We took a table and the girl went to the counter for our drinks, leaving her coat on her chair but taking her canvas tote with her. I tried to keep my eyes off her, turning to look out on the street, where the rain bucketed down and tree branches thrashed in the wind. In a few minutes the girl returned with our coffees and a plate of sticky buns on a tray. She took her seat and proceeded to dump two tubs of cream and three sachets of sugar into her coffee, stirring it with a plastic stick.

"Thanks," I said.

"*De rien*," she replied, taking a wolfish bite from a bun and licking brown sugar off her fingers as she chewed.

I drank in slow sips, watching her eat. The outfit she was wearing—rough, scuffed boots, cargo pants, the old T-shirt—emphasized her attractiveness, her lithe movements, her skin, eyes, hair. She was no runway queen, but she hadn't adopted the tough don't-mess-with-me style some girls favoured either. She had no visible piercings or tattoos. She was . . . herself, no phony act, no desire to please. I almost laughed. She was munching away, cheeks packed with raisin bun, and I couldn't keep my eyes off her. She drove ideas out of my head as soon as they formed.

She gulped down some coffee.

"So," she asked, "why *did* you warn me?"

"Warn you?"

"Yeah. At the art gallery that day."

"I don't know."

"Sure you do. You want the last raisin bun?"

"No thanks. Go ahead."

But she had already demolished a third of it.

"Anyway," I said, "I'll tell you if you tell me something first."

She licked her finger and ran it around the plate, chasing granules of sugar, then stuck the finger in her mouth.

"Depends what it is you want to know," she replied.

"Your name."

"Ninon. What's yours?"

"Julian."

She wiped her hand on her pants and held it out. "Pleased to meet you, Julian."

"Me too, Neen—er, sorry, how do you say it?"

"Ni-non. Like the joint in your leg plus *non*. It's a nick-name for Anne. So, getting back to my question and your evasive non-answer—"

How could I explain why I had alerted her to the guard who was watching her? Because she fascinated me—the smooth way she had slipped past the ushers, getting into the gallery without paying; the light-fingered theft of the woman's wallet; her bold reply to my lame pickup line? Because that day, as now, there was something about her, something exciting and mysterious that I couldn't explain to myself, let alone her?

I settled on a different answer, but a true one. "I didn't want to see you get caught. I knew they'd throw you between the gears."

She tilted her head. "Gears?"

"Yeah. The machine. They dump you in at one end and you never know when—or if—you'll ever come out again. The guard would have grabbed you, marched you to a little room with no windows and called the cops. You'd have been taken away in a cruiser to the cop shop. Forms would have been filled out and—"

"Okay, okay, I get it."

"I didn't want that to happen to you."

She looked straight into my eyes for a moment, then her glance slid toward the window.

"The rain's stopped," she observed.

"You're not like normal girls," I blurted. I hadn't been planning to say it. "I mean that in a nice way," I added hastily. "What I mean is—"

"Who wants to be normal?" There was no anger in her voice. "Anybody can be normal."

I laughed. "Then we have the basis for a beautiful friendship. I'm not normal either."

Ninon got to her feet, threw on her coat and picked up her tote. "I'd better go," she said.

"Wait! I . . . can we meet again? Soon?"

She turned toward the door. "If you want."

I followed her outside. "Where?"

The sun had broken through, illuminating the beads of rain on the overhead wires and leaves, the puddles on the sidewalk like sheets of glass. Ninon stood on the curb and nodded toward the park.

"Drop by. You'll find me there once in a while."

"But where do you live?"

She held up her index finger and revolved it slowly. "Around. Bye."

And she jaywalked across Dundas. I knew better than to follow her.

I jogged back to my apartment, shivering in the post-storm cool, with Ninon occupying my mind the way light fills a room. I couldn't stop thinking about her. I replayed our brief time together, tasting and retasting the memory while it was fresh, analyzing her words and the expressions that played across her features. And as usual I came to pessimistic conclusions: one, she only had coffee with me to thank me—pay me back—for helping her at the gallery that day; two, she wasn't interested in seeing me again.

Then I combed through everything I had said or done while we were together, like the ritual dissection of my performance after a game, searching for mistakes, the moves I could practice for next time. But I couldn't unsay my words to her, and it looked like there might not be a next time, so it was a depressing and useless exercise. What was there about Ninon that made me feel that I was about to cross a line and run heedlessly toward something new? I had been Mr. Careful for most of my life. Why was I ready—eager—to throw that away?

ELEVEN

THE NEXT MORNING I walked into the store to find Gulun in a turmoil, so upset he'd forgotten to knot his tie. There had been a recall order issued by the company that supplied our dairy products. Gulun ordered me to empty the coolers and haul every carton of milk, tub of yogurt, block of butter and wedge of cheese to the back room so the company truck could come and whisk it all away "before somebody got sick."

"What about the ice cream?" I asked. "It'll melt."

"Put it out in the alley. How I gonna make any money if I can't sell milk for two days?" he lamented.

"What's wrong with the stuff?"

"I dunno. A germ."

I set to work filling a cart with milk, lining up the containers neatly so they wouldn't fall off on the trip to the back room. On the back of each carton was the picture of the same missing person—a preteen girl—and the row of identical images looked like a strip of postage stamps. I wondered if the posters did any good.

While I was hard at work Curtis sauntered through the door and made his way to the coffee machine.

"Morning, Julian," he said.

"Hi."

Curtis poured his beverage, turned and leaned on the counter, idly staring at the faces with MISSING over their heads and the name of the sponsoring organization under their chins. When the cart was full I pushed it to the back room. By the time I came back to start on the yogurt and sliced cheese, Curtis had left.

At quitting time I slogged home and mowed the lawn and swept the clippings off the sidewalk and stowed the mower in the shed behind the garage. Then I changed and put in a ninety-minute run, exploring the streets to the east of the house. When I got back I showered, threw on some clean clothes and collapsed, pleasantly tired, into my easy chair and opened my book. Below me at Rawlins's place I could hear the faint, irregular notes of a suffering mandolin.

I read for a while and then got up and microwaved a frozen TV dinner and watched a soccer game while I ate. After the game was over I locked up and went to bed.

When I got to work next morning, Mrs. Altan handed me a note Curtis had left with her the previous afternoon. After lunch, I went to see him.

"Got a proposition for you, Julian. Well, it's just an idea at this stage," he corrected as I sat down. "But I've been going over the possibilities. It may not come to anything, but who knows?"

"Uh-huh."

"What do you know about missing persons?"

Red lights flashed in my imagination; bells clanged. For the second time since I'd met him, I thought Curtis might be onto me. I forced a blank look into my face, tried to dial down the panic.

"What do you mean?"

"Well, you're still a teenager. You must be aware that lots of adolescents are missing."

"I suppose," I replied, deciding I probably had nothing to fear after all. "But I don't know any, if that's what you're asking."

"No, no," he assured me. "I wasn't implying that you did. I'm just asking if you know anything about . . . the phenomenon."

"Not really."

"Well, believe me, there are thousands of them out there. A few organizations help parents to find them. They're all over the Internet. I gather they're not too effective, and neither are the cops."

Now he had me thinking about Ninon. Was she on a Missing Persons list in some police station?

"It's hard to find someone who doesn't want to be found, I guess."

"Exactly," Curtis replied, as if he'd moved a checker to the end of the board. He sat back and stared past me, out the window and onto the street. "All those poor parents, worried sick, terrified, imagining the worst."

And some of them not so poor, I thought, catching his drift, recalling his strange behaviour at the store yesterday morning, when he couldn't keep his eyes off the milk cartons.

There was no pity in his voice, no empathy. He said it like a man thinking, It's going to be minus thirty degrees today, and I sell overcoats. His next sentence confirmed my suspicion.

"Ever heard the expression 'Send a thief to catch a thief'?"

"Sure."

"Know what it means?"

"I'm not an idiot, Curtis."

He slipped on his smile. "Come on, humour me."

"You're thinking the best person to find a runaway teen is another teen. And you just happen to know one. Your comparison falls down, though, doesn't it?"

He raised his eyebrows.

"The saying should be 'Send a runaway to catch a runaway.' I'm not a runaway," I lied.

The smile widened. "No, you're certainly not an idiot. Which is why—"

"Yeah, I know. Which is why you want me to work for you."

We sat and looked at each other for a moment. Curtis picked up a pen and tapped it on the desktop. I didn't like what he was driving at. It was too close to home.

I said, "A lot of them don't want to be found—"

"Sure, but the parents—"

"They have reasons for running."

"But they're in danger. Some of them, anyway. You have to admit that. They know what they're running *from* but can't know what they're running *to*. And they find themselves in a mess—drugs, prostitution, custody. A few end up dead."

And they don't all have a little old Chinese grandpa

with an iron handshake and piles of money and lots of connections to back them, I thought. Curtis was partly right, I had to give him that. It was a stretch to believe he was genuinely concerned, but still.

"True," I admitted.

He rapped his knuckles on the desktop. "Exactly. See? We think alike on this."

I waited, then it came.

"What I was thinking, Julian, was this: I could maybe try to take on a few clients, parents at their wits' end. People who have tried the cops, the agencies, the posters on the street-light standards. I could talk to them, see, and hint that I know a sort of private investigator who would work on their behalf, a young man who knows the streets, the hangouts, the—"

I cut him off. "And you'd be misleading them. I don't know—"

"Okay, but your advantage is not what you know so much as what you're not—you're not a cop, not a social worker, not an official of any kind. Not an adult. You get the idea? You could talk to kids, ask questions, nose around, follow someone if you have to. You blend in. People your age will talk to you more readily than a person with a uniform or a degree in social work. You'd operate under the radar."

I saw what he meant. Kids clam up when asked to give info about another kid to an authority figure. It's something you don't do. You'd be breaking the strongest code there is.

"I get your point," I said. "But I'm not the guy you want. If by some miracle I found a runaway and if they

didn't want to go back home there's no way I'd turn them in, to you or anyone else."

Curtis put his elbows on the desk and linked his fingers under his chin. "Fair enough, Julian. Let's put it this way. If what you describe ever happens we let it drop and I tell the parents I failed to fulfill their hopes."

"I don't know. I'll have to think about it."

The truth was, I didn't have to think about it at all. I was a runaway myself, with phony ID in my wallet. Chasing stray teens would, sooner or later, drag me into contact with the very people I had to avoid if I wanted to be free— cops and social services. Curtis had said, "Send a thief to catch a thief," without thinking about what happens to the thief you send. When the job is done he's still a thief—and he goes right back to jail.

"Certainly," he replied. "Take a few days, more if you like, and let me know. But remember, we may have a chance to help someone."

I stood up. "Okay."

But he wasn't finished. "And—not that this should affect your decision—I'd be able to pay you more than last time. You did well then. You held up your end of the bargain. That's a rare quality in a person."

Sure, I thought.

"See you later," I said.

TWELVE

THE TROUBLE WITH THINKING about things is that most of the time it's impossible to turn off the flow of ideas. Curtis's proposition churned away in the back of my mind all evening. I polished off a new James Lee Burke, but even reading about the violent escapades of Robicheaux and his pal Clete couldn't capture all of my attention. I went on line and searched the local library's catalogue to see if I could find a Captain Alatriste story I hadn't read yet, but had no luck. I had to settle for a movie on TV, but it was boring so I went to bed.

Sleep was a long time coming. Sometime during the night I was awakened by the sound of a door closing at the back of the house. I sat up and eased out of bed and stood listening. The back door led from the downstairs hall into the garage. It was kept locked, and I thought I had the only key—on a hook inside my kitchen cupboard. There was no

movement above in Fiona's place, or below in Rawlins's apartment.

My bedroom window looked onto the fenced yard behind the garage. I peered out. There was no moon and the space was a pool of darkness. Nothing moved. I padded into the kitchen. The rear window was directly above the garage roof but allowed a partial view of the driveway, faintly illuminated by the street light across the road. There was a car parked there.

A figure in dark clothing and a baseball cap that hid his face came around the far corner of the garage, where there was an access door. I thought I had the only key to that one, too. When he opened the car door the interior light didn't come on. He slid into the driver's seat and closed the door quietly. The car started up, backed out onto the street and glided away. Only when it was almost out of sight did the headlights come on.

Chang had told me that the two downstairs rooms were used occasionally on a short-term basis. He had said that I should pay no attention if anyone turned up there. In other words, mind my own business, like Rawlins said.

But that didn't stop me from creeping downstairs, stealing along the hall past Rawlins's door and turning the handle on the entrance to the garage. It had been relocked. I stood in the shadowy corridor for a while, close to the doors to the two rooms. There was someone in the unit nearest the garage.

The car returned and left twice before first light. By the time I headed off to work in the morning, both rooms were occupied. As far as I could tell by lying on my kitchen floor, ear to the hardwood, the new guests were young women who spoke nothing but Chinese.

I never laid eyes on them. If Rawlins or Fiona noticed their presence they never mentioned it. Obviously Chang had the same understanding with all three of us. The women stayed four days, without, as far as I knew, leaving their rooms, then disappeared one afternoon when I was out looking for Ninon.

It was a little weird having transient boarders sneaking in and out of the house, dropped off and picked up by cars with their headlights turned off. It was like living over a bus station where only ghosts came and went. On Saturday Chang called and, after politely asking me how I was doing, requested that I go downstairs and clean the rooms thoroughly: wash the bedding, sweep the floor, toss the garbage, scour the bathrooms. All as soon as I could. He then, also politely, reminded me to ignore the guests' visit.

"Don't worry," I told him. "A deal's a deal."

I searched the park every day at least once but I didn't see Ninon all that week. Nor did I hear from Curtis. I plodded through my daily routines—calisthenics, breakfast, work, a long run—every day, enjoying my freedom from school, practices, games and meeting other people's expectations. On Saturday I ran along Bayview on my way back home, filmed with sweat, hungry and thirsty, looking forward to a shower and a coffee. I climbed the long hill out of the Don River valley, caught the light in time to cross Bloor and ran across the bridge under the anti-suicide fencing. On the Danforth I slowed and then stopped and looked at a window display that caught my eye every time I passed.

Three gleaming scooters stood there, as if waiting for me to pick one out, mount up and roar off into the distance. I had wanted a motorbike since I was about ten, one of the sleek, wickedly fast brands on the Grand Prix circuit, with their streamlined cowlings and fat rear tires and exotic foreign names. Nowadays I was more realistic. I'd settle for one like the green Italian model in the window, a stodgy, 150cc, practical scooter—used, not new. Someday, maybe.

I began to jog again and soon turned the corner onto my street, smiling to myself. I had a driver's license, courtesy of Bai and Chang, but I didn't know how to drive—a car or a scooter. But the real obstacle was money. I didn't have enough for lessons, let alone a scooter.

I had vowed that once Bai had given me my new identity and a place to live and a job, I wouldn't ask for anything more. The whole point in becoming Julian Paladin was to be someone new and to be in control of my life. I wouldn't go back with my hand out. I'd work for what I got. So I needed a job that paid more and gave me more hours.

In a way I wished I could agree to Curtis's scheme. I'd be able to bank enough cash to afford some extras. I decided I would keep working for him, but I'd draw the line at searching for runaways.

After dinner I rode the subway downtown and walked to Grange Park. It was a sultry evening and the air lay like stagnant water in the streets. The hot weather had brought people out of their buildings and into the park, and there was lots of activity of both the lazy and energetic kind. Shuttlecocks arced back and forth over the grass, Frisbees sailed past benches occupied by late shoppers resting their feet, parents chatted while kids played on the grass. I took a stroll around the grounds, looking for Ninon, and approached a clutch of black-clad, white-faced kids lounging under a tree.

"Hey," I greeted them.

A guy with a spiked mohawk replied, "Hey."

The rest of the group made a show of ignoring us.

"You seen Ninon around?" I asked.

"Who?"

"Sorry, I thought you might know her."

"'S'kay."

I moved on, sat on the end of a bench where a boy and a girl wearing school uniforms stared dreamily into the distance.

"Hey," I tried again.

The guy, a stocky redhead, turned in my direction. Even in the soft light of the evening I noticed his pupils were so dilated the irises had almost vanished.

"Hey," he replied, then let out a high-pitched giggle. The girl, who had been staring at the music player in her hand as if she couldn't figure out how it got there looked up, slowly focused on her friend and giggled even louder.

"Hey!" the boy said, and off he went again.

"Straw!" exclaimed the girl.

"Grass!" they pealed in unison, laughing so hard I thought they'd choke.

One last try. There were two black guys playing chess on the same table Ninon had been using when I found her writing in her notebook. They were dead serious, staring at the board while a double-faced chess clock ticked away between them. I watched them play. I'd seen them in the park before, once as part of a tournament. The taller of the two had three furrows etched across his brow, giving him a scowly look, which worsened as he nudged a black piece forward one square and slapped the stem on his side of the clock.

His opponent picked up his knight in his long fingers and thumped it down.

"Checkmate."

"Man, I give up," his opponent grumbled.

"*Pay* up, *then* give up."

Money changed hands and I saw my opening.

"You guys seen Ninon today?"

The winner looked lazily toward me, jamming his wallet back into his jeans. "And you are?"

"A friend."

"A friend with a name?"

"Julian."

"Ain't seen her for a while," he said, turning away.

His opponent was setting up the board for a new game.

"Do you know Ninon?" I asked, my words falling between them. "Can you tell me where I can find her?"

"You're white this time," the winner said to his friend, resetting the clock.

And Curtis wanted to pay me to interview people?

THIRTEEN

A FEW MINUTES AFTER I got home I heard a knock on my door. Fiona was standing in the hall, wringing her hands, her face flushed. She was wearing her nurse's uniform.

"Julian, thank God you're home," she gushed. "I hate to do this, I really do, but, really, I need to ask you a huge favour, I'm in a tight spot, just got a call from Trish, she's my daycare lady down the street, I think I told you about her, only she's had a bit of an emergency with her own wee one and she can't make it home for about two hours and—"

The flood of words stopped; Fiona took a breath.

"—and my shift starts in twenty minutes and I really, really can't afford the time off because it's an extra shift and it means overtime and I need the money, so would you, could you look after Roger for me?"

"Me? But—"

"Trish will be home as soon as she can to pick him up. She won't be long."

"Fiona, I don't know anything about babies."

"Aye, but he's asleep. If he wakes just give him his milk, it's all ready for him in his cup on the kitchen table, and put him in the playpen and—"

"But I might do something wrong. I might hurt him."

"Ach, you'll be fine. Please, Julian."

Ten minutes later I was in Fiona's place—which smelled of dirty diapers and fish and chips this time—and Fiona had sprayed me with instructions that streamed from her lips into one of my ears and out the other as she spun out the door like a uniformed dust devil.

I put my head around the door to her bedroom, feeling like an intruder. The room was more like an oversized closet, with space for a single bed—unmade—Roger's crib, and a rug and a small dresser against the wall between them. Roger lay scrunched up, his bum in the air, a bubble at the corner of his mouth, breathing deeply.

I made myself a cup of tea and sprawled on Fiona's lumpy sofa, afraid to turn on the TV and wake Roger. Instead, I thought about Ninon. Should I give up on her? One thing was sure: my search method wasn't working. I had been with her twice since the Van Gogh exhibit last March; once when she happened upon me on McCaul Street, the other in the park where I was looking for her. In other words, once by blind chance and once by design, and even the second was mostly luck. Fate and planning were tied.

My mistake, I decided, was in dropping by the park

once a day for a few minutes, a system that was statistically ridiculous. To boost the odds in my favour I had to spend more time there. A couple of hours, say. That was what I'd do. And if I was lucky and met up with her again and she took off without giving me a phone number or some reliable way to contact her, I'd give up on her. Maybe.

A murmur came from Fiona's room. I sat up, spilling cold tea down my shirt, and held still, afraid to make a sound. The murmur became a babble. The crib creaked. The babble shifted to a jabbering flow of non-words and the creaking intensified.

"Mama?"

I got up and crept into the room. Roger was standing in the crib, tiny hands clutching the rail, shaking the crib gleefully and talking a language only he understood. Then he saw me and shut down, his eyes widening in fear. And he bawled.

It took ten minutes of reassuring noises from me before Roger calmed down. I picked him up out of the crib and carried him into the other room and turned on the TV. When I put him in his playpen he threw back his head and howled some more.

"Okay, got it. No playpen."

I grabbed his plastic milk cup, with the kiddie lid that allowed him to drink without spilling, lifted him up again and sat on the couch with him after tuning the TV to a late afternoon hockey game. Roger drained the cup in no time, burped mightily and within a few minutes was fast asleep, his head on my shoulder.

The players were forming up for the third-period faceoff when I heard a key in the lock and the door opened to reveal an attractive, thin black woman with a baby in her arms. She looked at Roger and me.

"Awwww," she said.

Starting Monday I went straight to the park after work, postponing my run until later. I planned to stay for two hours each day. I read, watched a few chess games, walked around the block. It was boring. I sat and pretended I was doing surveillance for Curtis, singling out a person or couple and trying to draw conclusions about them from their clothing or actions. I made a dash to the restaurant and after Mrs. Zhu asked, "Eat in or take out?" I'd leave with a carton of whatever fried noodle dish was on the menu that day. She never let me pay.

"Mr. Chang say no," she reminded me firmly. On my second visit she commanded, "Not call me Missus. Call me Mama Zhu."

On Friday I was sitting on a bench between two chattering nannies, each with one hand resting on the handle of her stroller containing one sleeping kid. I had put in two and a half hours of the "Find Ninon" game and I was fed up with it. I was hungry and on edge. Grumbling to myself, I was leaning over, packing up my stuff and fishing in my pack for a subway token, when a shadow fell across the ground at my feet. I looked up.

It was Ninon. She had a talent for unexpected appearances.

She had traded the military outfit for jeans and a bleached-out long-sleeved shirt with a row of little flowers embroidered above the pockets. Her hair was loosely gathered behind her neck with a bit of string, her skin pale, her eyes dark with fatigue.

"What's new?" she said.

"Where have you been?" I blurted, not caring how unfriendly I sounded.

She frowned. "If we're going to be friends you won't ask me things like that."

I stood and shrugged into my backpack. "Are we?"

"Are we what?"

Throwing up my arms in frustration, I snapped, "Going to be friends!"

She took a step back. "We shook hands, didn't we?"

"Yeah, right. Didn't mean much, did it? Look, if you don't want me around you, just say so and put me out of my misery. This is driving me nuts."

She looked past me at something, then at my face.

"I do want you around," she said.

Shock displaced my frustration.

"Don't look at me like I tried to sell you a watch with no hands, okay? Let's start over." She held out her hand. "Hi, my name is Ninon."

I didn't take her hand. I said nothing.

"And you are?" she urged.

"Confused," I replied, slipping my hand into hers and holding it for a moment. "And hungry. Do you like spicy food?"

Mrs.—Mama—Zhu's round, passive face showed no reaction when I showed up at the restaurant with Ninon.

"Eat in, please, Mama Zhu," I said, beating her to the punch and leading Ninon to a table.

Ninon looked around at the faded prints of tigers and

peonies and fish tacked to the drab walls, and ignored the slurps coming from the table behind her, where a man sat hunched over his noodles. She fingered the white plastic film of the throwaway table covering. One corner—the right—of her mouth turned up in an ironic half-smile.

"You know how to show a girl a good time, don't you?" she said.

"I can recommend the soup. Or fried noodles. Anything else is new territory."

Ninon studied the card that she'd pulled from between the bottles of soy sauce and chili, then handed it to me.

"Can you help me with this?"

The entire menu was in Chinese.

"What do you feel like? I'm sure Mama Zhu can help us."

Fifteen minutes later there were three steaming platters of food between us, all served by Mama Zhu herself.

"She likes you," Ninon observed when Mama Zhu had returned to her stool behind the counter.

"What makes you say that?"

"I can tell."

Ninon ate like someone who'd been waiting a long time for a decent meal, and I kept right up with her. We didn't talk much.

"Fantastic," she said when we sat back, unable to pack away even one more spoonful of chicken with peanuts, vegetables with oyster sauce, or Szechuan shrimp. "My mouth feels like it's on fire."

"Great, isn't it?"

"Do you eat like this every day?"

"No."

"Well, thanks for bringing me here."

"No problem. We can come here again any time you want."

She looked at her watch. Oh-oh, I thought. Here it comes.

"I have to go," she said. "But I'm not running off this time. I really do have to be somewhere."

"And I shouldn't ask where."

A smile was her reply.

"And you meant what you said? Before, at the park?" I asked.

"Yes."

"Okay," I replied. I gathered what courage I could find and took a deep breath. "Here's the thing. I think we should spend the day together on Sunday. The weather forecast says sunny and hot. We can go to Centre Island for the day. Lie on the beach. Swim. Chase the geese. Get to know each other."

"Um—"

Before she could give me her usual vague reply, I cut in. "I'll be down at the ferry dock at twelve o'clock. I'll bring lunch. If you're there, great. If not, I'll eat all the sandwiches myself."

Every nerve in my body was firing at once as we left the restaurant and walked along the alley to Spadina.

"Thanks again. See you," Ninon said.

"Bye."

I watched her walking south, disappearing and reappearing in the Friday afternoon crush like a faulty bulb flashing on and off. And then, before I knew what was happening, I found myself striding in the same direction. I told myself I wasn't following. I was just taking an indirect route to the subway. She showed no sign that she knew I was behind her but, to be sure, I took a diagonal to the other side of the street at the first corner. With each cross street that appeared I told myself I would turn off Spadina, but I didn't.

At Queen Street, Ninon crossed Spadina with the flow of pedestrians, then stopped and looked west, one of a crowd waiting for the streetcar. Screened by a wall of bodies, I made my way to the south side of Queen, then stepped into the shadow of a music store doorway. I had a clear view of her across the road, waiting, talking to no one. I'd just stay put until she got on the trolley—sort of see her off.

It wasn't long before a streetcar came to a stop. She waited for the disembarking passengers to clear, then scooted up the steps. I could see her though the windows, standing by the token receptacle for a few seconds, then moving down the aisle. The light changed and the streetcar crossed the intersection.

At that moment a taxi pulled up to the curb right in front of me. A woman got out of the taxi, hung a purse on her shoulder and reached into the back seat for a brief-case. The streetcar rumbled past, no more than a few metres away. Its bell clanged. Before the woman could close the taxi door I slipped into the back seat.

"I know this is going to sound corny," I said to the driver, a wide-shouldered man wearing a knitted cap. "Follow that streetcar."

He studied me in the rear-view mirror.

"My sister's on it," I explained. "I forgot to give her something."

Slapping the car in gear, the man growled, "Whatever you say, chief."

The taxi crept along behind the streetcar, stopping at

every intersection to exchange passengers, waiting for the traffic light to change, moving off again. I'd have been just as far ahead to follow on foot. Every metre I travelled piled guilt on my shoulders. What was I doing? Things had just begun to look up for me and here I was invading the privacy that for some reason was so important to Ninon. Why couldn't I leave it alone?

To make things worse, the fare indicator on the meter rose alarmingly whether the taxi was moving or not. I'd be out of cash in no time at this rate. No, wait, I reminded myself. I had a credit card in my wallet. I only carried it for emergencies, and this was beginning to look like one. I sat back, relieved but sinking deeper into self-loathing, as the streetcar towed us into an increasingly downscale neighbourhood. Boarded-up storefronts. Discount stores. Rundown hotels and cafés. Lost-looking men and women on the sidewalks.

The streetcar came to a halt and I saw Ninon step down. "Here, pull up here," I told the driver.

I had just enough cash to cover the fare. I paid the driver, who muttered, "Say hello to your sister for me," before he roared off.

Ninon had turned the corner and set off down a side street. I waited a couple of minutes before following. She walked quickly along the sidewalk, about fifty metres in front of me. Farther along, a sign hung out over the doorway of a blank-faced brick building. A couple of guys and a woman stood smoking by the door under the sign. Without greeting them Ninon pulled the door open and went in. I stopped. From that distance I could just make out flaking black letters on a white background.

Guiding Light Mission and Hostel.

———

In a way, I wasn't surprised. From the beginning I had thought Ninon might be a "person of no fixed address," as they said in the cop novels. It was possible she went to the mission to visit someone. She might be a runaway. Maybe she was passing through the city, planning to head for Vancouver when the weather turned cold, like so many others.

What was the point of speculating? If she wanted me to know, she'd tell me.

But I could do a little digging. When I got back to my neighbourhood I dropped into the library to pick up something to read. At the NEW ARRIVALS shelf I read a few dust-jacket descriptions of the stories inside, selected a couple and headed toward the checkout. Then I got a different idea. I went to the research area, presented my card and used one of their computers to go on line and check out the Guiding Light Mission and Hostel. It was run by a non-religious organization—which surprised me, given the name of the place—and was supported by private funds and grants from city and provincial governments. Latest financial statement on request. Donations welcome. The mission offered counselling—mostly for addictions but also for job searches and, according to carefully worded statements, victims of abuse. You could sleep there and get a meal, both for a "nominal" fee, but you couldn't live there. There was a three-night limit. If you had no money you could work off the fees in the kitchen.

Probably Ninon could stay three nights, let a day pass, then go back for another stint. But where did she go in the meantime?

FOURTEEN

On Saturday Mrs. Altan asked me to work all day. Gulun had taken the train to Hamilton to visit his brother in the hospital.

"Leaving me with all the work," she complained.

I didn't object. More hours meant more pay.

He came back around five o'clock. On my way home I picked up sandwich fixings—Calabrian bread, cheese, ham, some fruit and apple juice. I had no idea what Ninon might like, so I guessed. I stowed the groceries in the fridge and went out for my run. After dinner I watched a remake of a movie based on Raymond Chandler's detective novel *The Big Sleep*. For some reason they moved the locale from LA to England. The book was better. I couldn't concentrate on the movie anyway. My stomach was in knots. Will Ninon show tomorrow? I asked myself every ten minutes.

In the morning I woke early, unable to sleep any longer. I built the ham-and-cheese sandwiches, pestering myself with questions I couldn't answer. Did she like mayonnaise? She must; everybody did. Should I trim the crusts from the sandwiches? No, leave them on. How about pickles? Didn't have any, and it was too late to zip out and get some.

I packed the sandwiches, along with a blanket for the picnic, sunglasses, a map of the Toronto Islands I had grabbed from the Web after breakfast, and some breath mints. All the while I hoped that I wasn't wasting my time. As time passed the butterflies in my stomach fluttered faster.

I timed my arrival at the ferry dock so I'd be there a half-hour early. I was off by fifteen minutes, which didn't leave much time. The quay was a madhouse. Mothers. Fathers. Dogs and beach balls and baby strollers. Kids with skateboards. More kids with kites, dolls, soccer balls that wanted to roll and bounce. I tried to find a vantage point to catch sight of Ninon when she arrived.

But she was already there.

She was sitting on a bollard at the edge of the quay, writing in her notebook, one ankle resting on the opposite knee, her canvas satchel at her feet. She seemed unaware of the chaos spinning noisily around her. I noticed that the blue beret was back. Behind her the calm water of the harbour stretched under a clear blue sky, the islands a lumpy green backdrop, the ferry about halfway across the lagoon, lumbering toward the dock, a V of foam at the bow.

"Hi," I greeted the top of Ninon's head.

She jotted down a half-dozen numbers, then marked her page with the ribbon, closed the notebook and secured it with the elastic band attached to the cover.

"Hi to you too," she replied, shoving notebook and pen into the satchel.

"I'll just go and get the tickets. We don't have much time."

"That's okay. I got them already," she said, and slung the bag onto her shoulder. "I didn't know there were three drop-off points, so I took a guess. Centre Island."

"That's fine. You look nice."

"I'm wearing the same clothes I had on the last time you saw me."

"Except for the beret."

"True," she conceded.

"And you do look nice. Again."

The ferry had bumbled into the slip, its reversed engines churning the water under the hull, and the crowd surged on board, impatient to begin the excursion. Jostled and bumped, Ninon and I went with the flow. We found an unoccupied spot on the bow rail. The ferry chugged across the lagoon, grey-brown water slipping under the hull below us. Seagulls wheeled overhead and alighted like a spray of confetti on the water in the boat's wake.

"Are you keeping a journal or something?" I asked, mostly for something to say. "Just wondering. I'm not trying to be nosy."

"Not really a journal, but similar. Just thoughts. Observations. Sometimes a sketch. You're staring at me."

"Sorry."

Her French accent, hardly noticeable, seemed to soften her speech. The sun brought out the auburn highlights in her hair, which hung thick and loose on her shoulders, contrasting with her green eyes and the blue of the beret. Who wouldn't want to look at her?

She pulled her notebook out of the satchel and opened pages at random, holding the book so I could see. Line after line of numbers, with the occasional sketch—a flower or two, a few faces, a narrow street.

"I write in code," she pointed out.

"Code? Why?"

"So no one—"

"So nobody else can read it. Right. Stupid question."

Two things were clear to me by now. Ninon was as nervous as I was. And I had learned more about her in the last ten minutes than she had revealed up until now. Why the sudden change in her? I decided not to waste time wondering.

"How does the code work?" I asked.

Ninon flipped to the last page of the notebook, fished a pencil out of her bag and printed the alphabet down the page, grouping the letters in columns.

"It's a really old code system," she explained, "called the Polybius square. You print the alphabet in a grid like this, five across and five down. I and J are treated as one letter. The code works when you add numbers—in this case, 1 to 5—along the top and down the side."

"Got it," I said. I didn't get it.

Ninon smiled her half-smile. "I haven't finished. The numbers can be written in any order you want, as long as the sender *and* receiver know what that order is. Watch."

She jotted the numbers down, but they weren't in sequence.

	5	2	3	1	4
2	A	B	C	D	E
1	F	G	H	IJ	K
5	L	M	N	O	P
3	Q	R	S	T	U
4	V	W	X	Y	Z

"Aha, now I *do* get it!"

"So what's the code for the letter A?"

"Um . . . fifty-two. Or twenty-five?"

"You use the top number first. What's V?"

"Fifty-four."

"And how do I write THE?"

"Thirteen, thirty-one, forty-two."

"Congratulations, you're officially a spy."

Ninon turned to another page, saying, "I keep a record of words I like."

I followed the movement of her finger as she read, "Andalusia. Conundrum. Toggery. Misericordia. Carpet-bagger."

"Even if you decode the numbers, I still don't know what any of them mean."

"It's not about the meaning; it's about the sound."

"The code seems like a lot of trouble to me."

She put her things in the bag. "When you've done a few sentences, the code begins to be automatic and it goes pretty quickly after that," she explained.

"Do my last name."

"You never told me what it is."

"Paladin."

Ninon smiled. "It means 'knight.'"

"Really?"

"King Charlemagne had twelve knights."

"Oh." As if I knew who he was.

I had picked my surname from an old black-and-white TV series I used to watch with Linda McCallum. *Have Gun, Will Travel* was a Western. The hero was a man dressed in black who packed a long-barrelled pistol in a leather holster with a horse's head shaped like a chess knight embossed on it. The man, whose business card said, "Wire Paladin, San Francisco," was a sort of detective and fixer who rode around helping his clients. Thanks to Ninon, I now understood the connection between the horse's head and the name.

"There are lots of ways to do the Polybius," she went on. "It's simple code. A cypher expert could crack it in no time. But the average person has never heard of it. I like codes."

And secrecy, I thought.

We turned and looked out over the water. Small boats, their sails drooping, struggled unsuccessfully to find enough breeze to move them along. The clamouring gulls escorted the ferry to the slip at Centre Island, the crew secured thick ropes around the bollards on the pier, the ramp was lowered and we followed the crowd onshore. It seemed like half the city had been struck by the idea of spending Sunday on the islands.

Ninon looked around. "I've never been here before," she told me.

"Me either." I reached into my pocket. "But I've got a map. What would you like to do first?"

"Walk," she replied. "Away from this crowd and this noise."

And so began the best day of my life.

———

We ambled along paths leading toward the eastern tip of the islands, then turned down a different trail heading back west, the air around us heavy with humidity and the odours of water and vegetation. Occasionally a whiff of candy floss or caramel corn or barbecue smoke drifted by. We weren't alone, but in a way we felt like we were, and our conversation was quiet and private.

The hot sun seemed to melt our shyness and coax uneasiness away, and gradually each of us opened the door into our lives and let the other in—a new experience for both of us. I told Ninon a lot of things about my past that I had never shared with anyone, but I held back everything about Mr. Bai and my new identity. I was Julian Paladin now.

For her part, Ninon unfolded much of her past, too. She had been born in a village called L'Isle-sur-la-Sorgue, in Provence, in the south of France.

"Where the sky is bluer than anywhere in the world," I said.

She nodded, then continued her story.

The village was an ancient community of stone buildings, cobbled streets, and a central square shaded by plane trees and anchored by a church. A village where everybody knew everybody else. What Ninon loved most about her birthplace, she said, was the river, the Sorgue, which was dammed at the eastern edge of the town and split into shallow streams that ran clear and pure around and through the village, turning the gigantic water wheels that used to power small factories. Ninon's father, Gilbert, was cook and bartender at the little Café France on the square. His food was famous in the area. The three Bissets lived in the apartment above Ninon's mother, Nathalie's, seamstress shop on the quay. Ninon did needlework for her mother to help out.

Ninon related all this as if it had been a dream. "And then everything went to hell," she said, almost whispering.

We had stopped for lunch, spreading the blanket in the shade of a beach umbrella. The sand was dotted with bathers. Kids dug in the sand and splashed at the edge of the water. Shrieks and laughter floated from the children's park behind us. We sat shoulder to shoulder, looking out at the undulating water stretching all the way to the horizon under the hammering sun.

Ninon continued her story. The event that began her nightmare was the move from Provence to Quebec City, where Gilbert's brother-in-law had invited him to come and take the chef's position in his upscale restaurant in the old town. Ninon was thirteen. She didn't like the city, hated the weather, made few friends, disliked the high school. She couldn't seem to adapt. They spoke a kind of French there, she said, but it wasn't like France at all. Nothing was.

One afternoon, when she was fifteen, her mother and father took her to her aunt and uncle's house, kissed her goodbye, and drove off to Montreal for the night to celebrate their wedding anniversary. It was the last time Ninon saw them alive.

"There was a shooting," she told me, hard-voiced and dry-eyed. "Some biker war. Retaliation for something. *Papa* and *Maman* were strolling down the street on the way back to their hotel after the celebration dinner. They got caught in the crossfire."

Ninon had no living relatives other than the aunt and uncle in Quebec City. They adopted her. Not long after, she took off and never went back.

I wanted to ask her why, but from personal experience I knew the question probably wouldn't be welcome. It could have been any of a dozen reasons. I kept silent. Then, after a few minutes I asked, "Were they nice?"

"My aunt was okay."

"But not your uncle."

She gave me a look that said more than her words. "He was too nice."

"Oh."

"And my aunt knew. And did nothing."

I shook my head. Sometimes there's nothing you can say.

"Anyway," she murmured, "now there's just me."

"Not anymore," I said.

We packed up our picnic and made our way slowly to the western beach. Ninon wanted to watch the sunset. Clouds were gathering, and the lowering sun set them on fire. We spread the blanket at the edge of the water. The still air remained hot and clammy. Around us adults collected kids, umbrellas, buckets and shovels and all their picnic jumble, then trickled away toward the ferry dock. By dusk we had the beach to ourselves.

We didn't talk much, as if the unfamiliar sharing of our past experience had used up all our words. Ninon yawned.

"Aren't you tired?" she said, curling up on the blanket and pillowing her head on her hands.

"Not really."

She didn't notice my reply. Her deep breathing and the sigh of the water brushing the sand were all I heard. I sat beside her, my hand on her shoulder. I didn't think she'd mind.

For a couple of seconds earlier in the afternoon, while Ninon was telling me about her life, I had envied her. She had relatives. She knew where they lived. She had memories of the place where she had been born and spent her childhood. Good memories.

But her aunt and uncle, especially her uncle, had betrayed her. I had no relatives that I knew, but I held no bitterness about my family either. How could I, when I knew nothing about them? Did they all die? Did they stick me in a basket and deposit me on some doorstep? Was I some sixteen-year-old's nightmare, given away? Maybe it was better not to know. Were fond memories of home just a mockery when you couldn't go back? I had suggested to Ninon, maybe you'll go back to Provence someday.

"I hope God heard that," was all she said.

After all the light had faded from the sky I lay down next to Ninon, her back against my chest, her head under my chin, and covered us as well as I could with the blanket. Her slender body was warm and moved rhythmically as she breathed. Her hair smelled of sunlight. I held her that way for a long time. In the sky above the water heat lightning flickered behind the massed clouds like fireflies in the dark.

PART THREE

MARIKA

. . . and then, 'stead of taking to the woods when I run off, I'd go down the river . . . and camp in one place for good, and not have such a rough time. . . .

—Mark Twain, *Huckleberry Finn*

FIFTEEN

I WAS LATE FOR WORK Monday morning, skulking through the door under Mrs. Altan's steely eyes and Gulun's black scowl. He grumbled a promise to dock my pay. I didn't care; I was riding high after my day with Ninon even though there had been a small glitch when we parted at the ferry dock earlier that morning. The sky had cleared overnight and the morning breeze was cool and clean. I asked if we could meet in the afternoon and she gave me one of her slippery replies.

"I don't want to smother you," I reassured her. "I had a good time yesterday."

"Me too," she replied, her eyes shifting to the side.

"So. Meet you at the park? Maybe?"

"Okay. But not today."

"Can I give you my address?" I asked her.

"Um, not right now. But I'll see you soon."

I figured Ninon was reluctant to be pinned down because she didn't want me to know she was living—at least most of the time—at the mission. I forced myself to be patient, not to push her. If I put pressure on, she might disappear for good.

But it was frustrating. There was no method to contact her. I had a phone now but was only allowed to use it for Chang business. Besides, if I called the mission she'd know I was aware that she stayed there.

I was stacking canned vegetables on the shelves near the street door when Gulun's stony words interrupted my thoughts. "You gonna daydream or you gonna work?" he shouted from the cash register.

"I am working. What do you want me to do?"

"I want you not be late!" he yelled, louder.

I stood up and walked to the counter, where he was jamming lottery tickets into the pockets of a display.

"How about not screaming across the store at me, okay? I said I was sorry for being late. I'll stay a couple of extra hours today."

"Words don't mean nothing," he snapped.

I turned back to work, holding in my anger, slashing open a carton with my box cutter. I whacked the cans onto the shelf, label to the front. Neat rows. When I had emptied the last carton I hauled it and the other empties to the back room.

Wearing a dark cardigan, Mrs. Altan was sitting at a small table she sometimes used as a desk, jotting numbers into a ledger with a stub of pencil. When I tossed the cartons to the floor she looked up from her accounts.

"Don't be angry at him," she said.

Her face, on most days creased by anxiety, seemed soft-ened, even sad. I didn't reply to her.

"You remind him of our son," she said.

Does he yell at him, too? I wondered.

"I didn't know you had a son."

The Altan family was a closed book to me. They could have had a dozen relatives stashed in the upstairs apartment for all I was aware, although even one extra person would have stretched the place to its limits. The apartment was the same size as the store.

"When we leave Turkey," Mrs. Altan replied, "our son stay behind with my sister's family until we can get a start here. Gulun don't want to leave him but I say it will be alright. We come first, save our money. But when the time come and we send for him it's too late. The rules all differ-ent. His papers expired and now he might have to go in army. He's big young man, strong, your size, also your age. Eighteen."

I nodded. I wasn't eighteen but Julian's birth certificate said I was.

"And he is our only child," she added. She sighed, straightened her back. "You are good boy, Julian. We know."

I went back to work, sweeping out the store and, for good measure, the sidewalk in front. When I stepped back inside Gulun was ringing up a sale. The customer brushed past me as Gulun recited his customary "Thanks. Come again."

I stood in front of the counter. When Gulun turned my way I said, "I apologize for being late. And I'm sorry about your son."

Gulun's face went blank. He swallowed. Then his chin began to quiver.

"God willing, you will meet him someday," he said quietly. "Here."

And just as quickly he composed himself. "I forget to tell you," he said, businesslike again. "Mr. Curtis ask me to say go and see him today if you can."

Curtis was on the phone when I got to his office. He uttered a long sentence sprinkled with legal terms I didn't understand, then dropped the handset into its cradle.

"Thanks for dropping by. Good weekend?"

"Fine."

"You're looking hale and healthy."

I couldn't think of anything other than "You too."

He put his smile on. "Interested in a little job?"

It didn't take him long to scare up a client with a missing kid, I thought.

"Depends."

"Always the cautious one," he commented after a forced laugh.

I figured I'd cut him off before he started the sales pitch. "I've thought it over. I can't help you find runaways."

"Run . . . No, no! This is something else. But what we talked about before—your youth—will still be a key advantage here, too. That's why I thought you'd be the ideal person."

That took me by surprise. "Oh," I managed.

"Let me fill you in, see what you think. What do you say?"

I nodded.

"Okay, here it is. Do you know what a peace bond is?"

"Somebody can't go near somebody else, and if he does, the cops pick him up."

Curtis was nodding.

"If they're not too busy," I added.

This time his chuckle was genuine. "Exactly! Which brings me to the job. A peace bond is imposed by a judge if the court thinks an individual is a threat to another individual. In this case the parents of a young woman are concerned their daughter's ex-boyfriend may hurt her. They persuaded her to swear out the bond. Apparently he has a history of abusing her—verbally and, at least once according to the father, physically. Hence the bond, and the parents' concern. Clear so far?"

"Crystal."

"Now, here's where it gets a little complicated. The young lady is over eighteen. This means that, legally, this is all none of her parents' business, so to speak. Therefore we need to remember: it's mom and dad who came to me for help and retained me, not the woman. I got the impression from them that she wouldn't be too grateful for their role in this."

"Retained you. That means hired you, right?"

"Yes."

"What's the daughter's attitude? How will she react if she finds out her parents are interfering?"

"She mustn't find out."

"But isn't she the one to choose the best way to handle the problem? It's her life. It's—he was—her boyfriend."

"All true, Julian. All true."

"So . . ."

"The parents think she's being naive. Given enough time, they believe, he'll hurt her, or worse. God knows there're lots of examples in the news every week. Are you aware that most murdered women are killed by men they know? And many or most of those men had once had a relationship with the woman they attacked?"

"No, I wasn't," I admitted. "Listen, if this is so serious why bring me in? I don't know anything about all this stuff. I can't be a bodyguard."

Curtis held up his hands, palms outward, as if to ward me off. "Whoa, Julian. You've got the wrong end of the stick. You'd do one thing and one thing only: track the guy and if he gets close to her—"

"Take pictures."

"Exactly. Don't interfere. Don't intervene. Don't let either of them know you're on the scene. And if this guy tries to hurt her, call 911 like any citizen would. Just make sure you remain undercover."

"What good would photos be?"

"They'd be ammunition I can use on behalf of the parents to get the cops to bring the guy in. See, a peace bond is a legal document. If the guy breaches the conditions, that's a crime, and anyone can report a crime. If someone reports on the parents' behalf, that adds weight and the police will have to move quickly. We hope."

"Okay, I get it."

"So you'll help?"

"I guess so."

"Excellent."

Curtis made to stand.

"But I have a condition."

He sat back down, spread his hands. "Okay, shoot."

"I want a smartphone I can keep, not a loaner. Registered

in your name, paid for by you. Second, I need you to set up a dedicated e-mail address that can't be traced to me. I'll send any photos I get to there, then erase them from the phone."

Curtis thought for a moment. "That's all?"

I nodded.

"Done. I'll courier the phone and background information on the young man and woman to you tomorrow."

In the subway en route to Grange Park I thought about the job I'd accepted—following a stranger and documenting him if I found him near his ex-girlfriend. Technically, I supposed, he'd be violating the bond even if he got close enough to call out to her. He didn't have to do anything. I wasn't blind to the fact that not long ago I tailed Ninon after she made it clear she didn't want me to know where she was going or where she lived. No, I hadn't threatened or abused her. I cared about her, but still. It was a betrayal of trust. My gut burned with shame. I almost left the train to go home, but I kept my seat, captured by thoughts of Ninon and the scent of sunlight on her skin.

"I'm getting a cellphone soon," I told Ninon, omitting the fact that I already had one.

We were sitting on a bench in Grange Park, eating ice cream cones—chocolate for me, butterscotch for her—and trying to stay ahead of the effects of the heat, our fingers gooey, the little napkins that came with the cones a soggy mess.

"Oh," she replied, devoting her attention to the ice cream running across her knuckles.

"Yeah. I'll give you the number and you can call me. If you want to, that is."

"Okay."

She tossed her sodden napkin into the bin beside the bench and began to suck on her fingers. "There's a Monet exhibit at the gallery soon."

"Who?"

"He was an Impressionist."

A dim light glowed briefly in my brain. "Oh, like Van Gogh."

"Vincent was a *Post*-Impressionist, but close enough. Anyway, want to come?"

"Definitely."

Ninon slung on her bag. "Good. It opens next Sunday. Now, I gotta go. Thanks for the cone."

"This time," I joked, "maybe you should buy a ticket."

She gave me a lopsided smile. "It's free on Sunday."

SIXTEEN

WHEN I WENT TO BED that night my room was hot and close. Rainfall woke me, a steady whisper at my open window, a hushed gurgle in the eavestroughs. I lay on my back, wondering what had disturbed my sleep. Then I focused on it: the hiss of tires on the wet road outside. The vehicle slowed and turned into the driveway below. The engine died. Doors opened and closed with the minimum of noise.

Quickly I crept out of bed, pulled on my shorts, tiptoed to the door of my apartment. I let myself out and stole down the stairs and sat on the third step from the bottom. Anyone who came in through the door to the garage wouldn't see me. But I'd hear them.

A moment later, a key in the lock. Whispering, in Chinese. Two men and a woman. The doors to the single rooms opened and closed softly. Likewise the entry back into the garage. A moment later, out in the driveway, the car started up, reversed, drove away. It was all over in minutes. I waited awhile, then stole down the hallway and stood still. A line of light under each door, a few thumps, a toilet flushing. Then nothing.

No further ahead, I padded upstairs and went back to bed.

In the morning I got up an hour earlier than usual and took the hoe from the toolshed in the yard. The ground under the windows of the downstairs rooms didn't really need reworking, but the new guests wouldn't know that. The morning sun sparkled on the wet grass; the air smelled of blossoms and rain. I hummed and whistled, hoping to attract attention, to see a curtain move, a face in a window. After almost an hour of completely unnecessary work and bad music I was rewarded.

A disembodied hand appeared, gripping the edge of a curtain, which unhurriedly moved aside. In the gap, most of a face, enough to show a long braid of black hair, a broad forehead and a bandage covering a swollen nose. Then face and hand disappeared as the curtain fell back into place.

Satisfied that I'd see no more, I put the hoe away and headed off to the QuickMart.

Around mid-morning a bicycle courier pushed through the door of the store, put a fat lumpy envelope on the counter and asked for a signature. It was from Curtis. I carried it to the back room and laid it on the table without opening it, enjoying the frustrated curiosity Gulun was trying mightily not to show.

I got home at the usual time, took a quick sneak along the downstairs hall on the off chance I'd see or hear something. A waste of time. In my kitchen I made a sandwich, poured myself a glass of orange juice, then sat down and slit the package open with my box cutter. A smartphone tumbled out—scratched and obviously used—along with a charger and fresh SIM card. There was also a file folder. Curtis had put together a dossier including notes and photos of both Marika and the ex, Jason Plath.

After inserting the card, I plugged in the charger and left the phone on the kitchen counter. I opened the folder, put aside the pics and began to read. Marika Rubashov, age nineteen, university student in the faculty of pharmacology, presently enrolled in summer courses to speed up her journey toward a degree. Broke up with Jason just after Christmas. Plath was at a community college in the city: computer repair, which the course catalogue described as computer "engineering."

The peace bond had been issued a little more than a month ago, around five months after the breakup that Plath would not accept. He had defied the order twice but Marika Rubashov hadn't informed the police. Why not? I wondered as I munched the last of my sandwich.

In his notes Curtis reminded me that he had been retained by Rubashov's parents, not Marika herself, and Marika didn't know that. Obviously, Curtis added, as if I couldn't have figured it out for myself, Plath didn't either.

In her photos, Marika was dark-haired, average height and build, not pretty but not plain. Her closed-in facial expressions suggested shyness, or maybe a lack of confidence. Plath was blondish, rail thin, tall. His long face wasn't exactly sunny. In all three of the pics he looked as if he thought the photographer was putting one over on him.

I bundled up the photos and papers, stuffed them back in the envelope and went for a run. While I loped along the hot streets south of my neighbourhood I worked out a plan for my new task and came up with an idea. I stepped inside a little café and used the public phone to call Curtis. When he answered I told him I needed a copy of Marika's course schedule at the university.

"You're supposed to watch *him*, not *her*," he objected.

"The easiest way to catch him harassing Marika is to watch *her*."

There was a pause. "Good point. I'll get you the schedule."

When I ran I'd normally fall into a rhythm and lose track of time, floating along with my thoughts, and today was no different. But my thoughts were prickly. Working out my method of observing Jason's behaviour led me to wonder what kind of jerk pesters a girl who has already broken up with him. Okay, breaking up hurts; everybody knows that. You might try to put things back together but eventually you have to face facts. Hanging around someone who doesn't want you there is pathetic.

Was it me rather than Jason I was thinking about? Was I the fool?

Before I knew it I was close to home. I slowed, jogging loosely to cool down. My tank top, drenched with perspiration, clung to my torso, and sweat trickled from the tips of my hair onto my ears. The unshaded stretches of the road surface shimmered with heat, and sunlight splintered on the windows of parked cars.

I turned onto my street about a block north of the house. In the distance, a couple of guys bounced a basketball back and forth, making their way up the centre of the road. Nearer the house they broke off and cut between the cars standing along the curb. One of them bungled his pass and the ball, on the rise from the bounce, thumped the grille of a small hatchback. There was a man in the driver's seat of the car, a newspaper spread across the steering wheel. The ball players laughed and carried on up a driveway.

Something about the scene wasn't right.

Instinctively I jogged past my house, eyes front, and turned onto the first side street I came to. I circled around and came at the house from the back, slipping up the driveway and entering the garage, then the door into the downstairs hall.

There were two things wrong with the street scene, now that I'd had time to think. The man hadn't reacted when the basketball struck his car. He hadn't even looked up. Second, the car windows were up and the engine wasn't running—therefore, neither was the air conditioner. Who sits in a closed car on a hot day reading the paper?

In my apartment I avoided the front window. I took a shower, dressed, slipped along the living room wall and peered around the window frame. The man was still there. He was clean-cut, Asian, mid-thirties, wearing a light blue golfing shirt. He had a clear view of the house from his vantage point—which didn't mean, I told myself, that he was staking out this particular place. But what if he was? I carried a chair from the kitchen to the window, then got a pencil and my notebook from my desk. I jotted down his license plate number, and the exact time and date. Should

I call Chang? Would he think I was silly? Imagining things? I settled in to watch.

Less than an hour later the man held a cell to his ear, then closed it, folded up the newspaper, started the car and drove away. He must have been a slow reader. He hadn't turned the page even once.

Curtis brought Marika Rubashov's class schedule next morning when he came into the store for his coffee and newspaper. I checked it over and found I had time to swing past Grange Park on my way to the university that afternoon. Marika had a class that ended at two o'clock. I set off from the store after work with my new cell and a map of the campus in my backpack.

I was beginning to feel like I was in the middle of a penalty-killing scenario with my team two men short, buzzing all over the ice, now here, now there, harassing and forechecking. I was searching for Ninon. I had to monitor a guy I'd never met who wouldn't leave his ex-girlfriend alone. There were night visitors drifting in and out of the house, and now a possible mystery with the watcher in the car.

Was there a connection between the watcher and Mr. Bai? His insistence on secrecy I could understand. So far, I had put it down to his not wanting to be discovered as the man who arranged my new identity—with documentation that was both false and illegal. At first I hadn't thought through all the details of my disappearance. I realized that I had burdened him with a huge responsibility. But who or what was he? A businessman for sure. Wealthy? Definitely. A crook of some kind? I had to admit the answer to that one was, possibly. Especially if I included the kidnap attempt by "business rivals." But I pushed that thought aside. Bai had an iron code of honour or obligation—whatever the right word was. He thought he owed me. He had kept his promise. So I had to keep mine.

And what explained the secret, dead-of-night comings and goings? Who were the women and occasional man who came and went like fugitives in some kind of underground railway? People have reasons to travel in the shadows: they're escaping danger or the past, or the law. I knew. I was one of them.

When I got to Grange Park, Ninon was nowhere to be seen. I backtracked north to the legislature buildings, which were situated in the middle of the campus, then I walked through an underpass toward my destination. I had never been on a university campus before. It was like entering a city within a city, with stretches of green lawn, old buildings of grey stone blackening from air pollution, newer structures, an ancient clock tower, a few aged trees. People who seemed full of purpose hurried along the sidewalks; others sprawled on the grass or sat in small groups, talking casually.

I found Marika's building and entered through the pointy-arched doorway into a wood-panelled hall. The classroom I was looking for was on the ground floor and easy to find. I sat down on a bench along the hall from the double doors. Around me students swept past, backpacks on one shoulder, earbuds in place. I checked out their clothes, pleased to find that, even though mine were downscale, I didn't stand out too much. I pulled out my novel and settled in to read, glancing toward the classroom doors every few minutes, Joe College taking a summer course, waiting for his pal and learning up a storm in the meantime.

But I wasn't Joe College and never would be. I wondered how my life would have unfolded if things had been different. If I'd had parents who wanted to put me through university and had the money to do it. Where would I be right now? In this same hallway? In a classroom, on my way to becoming a doctor or engineer or teacher? On the subway, my backpack full of books and assignments, heading home to a nice room, looking forward to seeing my parents and maybe a brother or sister around the dinner table?

I found myself aching for something I'd never had, and I felt a familiar emptiness, as if a part of me was missing. I hadn't even laid eyes on Marika yet and already, in a way, I envied her.

Five minutes before the hour I put my book away and stood against the wall, ready to move when I had to. Soon the doors opened and a stream of students poured out as if escaping a fire. In the corridor echoing with voices and the shuffling of feet on the polished floors it wasn't easy to examine faces rushing past, but I soon caught sight of Marika.

She was wearing jeans, a dark blue sweatshirt with the university logo on it and canvas boating shoes, walking alone toward the arch of sunlight at the open door. Once outside, she wasted no time. I followed her past the clock tower and along Hoskin Avenue toward the subway stop at the Museum.

Her body language practically shouted: eyes down, shoulders hunched, fingers hooked under the straps of her leather backpack. She avoided eye contact with other pedestrians.

On the subway, the same. When we reached her stop I tailed her out to the street, then through a leafy neighbourhood north of Lawrence, keeping my distance. Eventually she disappeared into a two-storey brick house with stained-glass trim above the bow window.

On my way home I logged my time and a quick account of my afternoon in my notebook. Then I sat like the other passengers, staring into the double world of train windows reflecting the car's interior—the ads on the walls, passengers sitting and standing—overlaid by the image of the dark tunnel and lights flashing past.

Marika, I thought, seemed defeated. You could see it in the timid way she scurried home, as if she wasn't safe until she got through the door. Had she been born that way, or had Jason Plath robbed her of any confidence and optimism she might have had? Was he like some guys I had met on and off the ice, people who pushed through life with a lit fuse, violence lurking just below the skin?

I decided to put as much time as I could into Marika's case between now and my Sunday visit with Ninon. Back home I checked out a few social media sites that she used, according to info her parents had given Curtis, hoping to find something useful. No luck.

After dinner I took a walk up to a food market on the Danforth. The day's heat lingered in the pavement and seeped from the buildings, and the sidewalk patios were going strong.

I left the market weighed down by two bulging plastic bags and a full backpack, vowing not to let my food supply get so low again—a promise I had made to myself before. The Danforth had settled into a steady rhythmic hum, a peaceful contrast to the frantic daytime bustle. My street was quiet, the street lights flickering to life in the dusk, throwing the shadows of trees across the road.

I almost missed the stakeout. It was a different car this time, parked facing south, but once again with a clear view of my house. I reminded myself that the man in the car could also observe a half-dozen other houses from where he sat, that there was nothing to prove my house was his objective. But I memorized the plate number anyway.

I sauntered past as if I hadn't noticed him. Another Asian, taller than the first one, sitting with his head back, the smoke from a cigarette curling to the ceiling. I turned up my sidewalk, strolled through the pool of darkness under the oak, up onto the verandah and through the door. I turned on my living room light, went to the kitchen and put away my groceries. In my notebook I jotted down the time and the stakeout car's license plate number.

Two Asians hanging around outside my place went way beyond probabilities. Police? What were the chances that two different plainclothes city cops staking out the same neighbourhood would be Asian? If not cops, who? Were they in any way connected to Bai or Chang? Could they be the "business rivals" Chang had vaguely mentioned when I asked him who had tried to snatch Wesley?

I picked up the Chang phone, set to show Unknown Caller and to block my own number, and punched in the memorized number.

"It's Julian," I announced, and relayed my telephone number.

Chang called back five minutes later. I related the details of the two different watchers in two different cars, wondering if Chang would conclude that I was losing my brains.

"I'm not sure if it's this house they're watching," I added. "Do you want me to go down and speak to the guy? I could—"

"No. Do nothing. I will deal with this."

"Okay."

"You did well to call, Julian," he said, and clicked off.

Chang hadn't seemed surprised by my information, but then nothing seemed to ruffle him. He seemed to accept as a fact that it was my house the watchers were scoping out, so I supposed I should too. I turned on the lamp beside my reading chair by the bow window, opened the sash and picked up my book—coincidentally a cops-and-robbers thriller set in the city where at this very moment I was pretending not to notice the guy smoking in a car on the street outside my house. The watcher had opened a newspaper, folding it lengthwise against the steering wheel. He sat there, not reading and pretending not to watch the house while I sat not reading and pretending not to watch him. It was funny in a way.

Nothing happened.

Why the stakeout? Only one answer came to mind. The mystery guests. Who were they?

The only thing I knew for certain was that I didn't know anything for certain. Except one fuzzy detail: everything seemed to originate with Mr. Bai, who was more of a puzzle than ever.

———

Over the next few days every minute of my life was full—mostly with the Marika job. Before heading to the university in the afternoons, I varied my appearance. Sometimes I took a different backpack; always I carried a couple of baseball caps with me, switching them as I followed my quarry along the streets. Most days I took a reversible shell for variety. But for all I had gained by the end of the week I might as well have stayed home and knitted a sweater.

Plath never turned up. Marika plodded through the routines of her school day. I watched her house after dark each night, at random times, but if she was sneaking out it must have been through a window and down a fire escape. I was on the verge of going permanently insane from boredom.

Curtis's notes said she spent a few hours at the local library on Saturdays. Worth a try. When she emerged from her house in the morning I was ready. I tailed her through the streets, noting that the upscale neighbourhood lost its shine after a few blocks, and followed her into an old stone library set in a grove of maple trees. Marika headed straight for the computers and sat down and shoved a card into a reader attached to the machine. I cut off to the side and took the staircase to the mezzanine, where I was able to observe her while pretending to glance through books on farming in the Early Middle Ages.

Soon Marika logged off and disappeared into a different room. I found her at a quiet area in the stacks by a window, where a couple of work tables had been set up. Through three ranks of bookshelves I watched her unload texts and a notebook from her backpack, along with a laptop, and set to work.

I left the library and found a bench in a parkette across

the road where I could keep an eye on the library doors. I switched caps and put on a pair of sunglasses. It was hot, even in the shade of the spindly little trees planted in the dry ground around the bench. I yawned. My mind drifted, gravitating to Ninon and our upcoming meeting at the gallery the next day. I hadn't seen her in almost a week. I hoped she wouldn't retreat to the don't-ask Ninon of the past.

She was unlike any girl I'd ever met and she held my attention like a magnet. She was pretty, smart, mysterious, unafraid—her own person. How different from the timorous, closed-in Marika, soldiering away on her laptop in the library.

"Hey, wait a minute!" I said out loud, startling the hungry pigeon stalking toward me.

Why would someone with a laptop in her pack bother to use the library's computers?

"For two reasons," I told the pigeon. "One: she wanted no record on her laptop of any websites she may have visited or e-mails she may have sent. Two: her parents were in the habit of snooping in her laptop—and she knew it."

The pigeon was so impressed it flew away.

SEVENTEEN

THE MONET EXHIBIT was scheduled to open at ten
o'clock. When I got to the art gallery at a quarter to, there
was already a lineup in the shade of the massive glass and
steel overhang. I joined the queue and kept watch for
Ninon, recalling the day at this same place when I had first
laid eyes on her blue beret. As soon as an usher unlocked
the doors, the lineup began to ooze forward. A man ahead
of me explained to his partner that, because the exhibit was
in high demand, the gallery let only a limited number of
patrons in at fifteen-minute intervals. I craned my neck,
searching the street in both directions.

My anxiety escalated as I shuffled closer to the entry
doors. Soon I was standing in the cool subdued lighting of
the atrium, fidgeting. The queue progressed. Conversations
spun around me. At last, nearly frantic, I found myself a few
feet from the roped divider that formed the entrance. I'd

have to go in next or go to the end of the line and start over.

Then Ninon burst through the glass doors. She was wearing leather sandals, tight white capri pants and a red T-shirt. Her trusty carryall drooped from her shoulder. Her thick hair hung loose, framing the oval face with the green eyes. Definitely worth the wait. I noticed that a couple of the men in line thought so too.

She rushed over to the coat check to store the carryall.

A voice behind me muttered, "Excuse me?"

I turned, blank-faced, to see a well-dressed older woman, her face pinched with impatience.

"Are you going in?" she demanded.

I looked at a lot of paintings that day, but not much registered, just framed blurs of colour and light—fields with poppies, lily pads on the surface of a pond, sunrises, sunsets. As if parched, Ninon drank them all in. I drank her in. Beside her, poor Monet didn't stand a chance. She told me about his brush technique, his use of colour, his composition, and I floated along on the gentle current of her voice.

"Did you study art at school in Montreal?" I asked.

"No, in Provence."

"Where the sky—"

"You're beginning to repeat yourself," she said, grabbing my hand and dragging me across the room. She stopped at a picture showing a woman in a long white dress, standing on a hill, struggling to hang onto a green parasol. Her blue scarf snapped in the wind, the grass golden at her feet, a cloud-bunched sky behind. Ninon studied her for a long time.

Then she turned to me and said, "She looks like she wants to grip her parasol in both hands and step off that hill and let the wind sweep her away."

"Away where?"

"Home."

Home to Ninon wasn't Montreal and it certainly wasn't the Guiding Light Mission. It was L'Isle-sur-la-Sorgue. I took her hand, hoping she'd understand why. She squeezed mine and we meandered through the rest of the exhibit. Sooner than I wanted, we came to the end.

Out on the sidewalk the harsh noontime sun hammered the pavement, and the baked air smelled of car exhaust.

"Hungry?" I asked.

She nodded. "Should we go to that Chongqing place?"

"If you'd like."

In the unforgiving light of a hot afternoon, Ninon's clothing, although clean, looked well worn. The hem and collar of her T-shirt had been restitched, the thread colour not a perfect match, and an odd button had been sewn onto the left leg of her capri pants where there was a small V on the cuff at mid-calf. She had learned a lot from her seamstress mother, all right.

Mama Zhu greeted us with a stern mini-lecture on the theme of staying away too long before she took us to the back of the little restaurant and set us up at the table I had used on my first visit there. She shouted, "*Cha!*" at the kitchen door, then said to Ninon, "You got to eat more. You got no colour."

Mama Zhu was right. I hadn't noticed it so much at first sight that morning or in the muted lighting of the gallery, but Ninon seemed pale, with the beginnings of darker circles under her eyes. She looked tired. Maybe it was hard to get a good night's sleep at the mission, surrounded by strangers coughing, mumbling, crying out in their sleep.

Our tea arrived and I poured us each a cup of the green jasmine-scented liquid.

"*À votre santé*," Ninon said, clinking her cup against mine.

"Got something for you," I announced, handing her a piece of paper. "My cell number."

"Okay," she replied, and stuffed the paper into her satchel.

Food arrived: steamed rice, oval plates of beef in black bean sauce, chicken with cashews, heaps of green vegetables, curried shrimp.

"I don't remember ordering these," Ninon said, drawing in the fragrances with deep breaths.

"I think Mama Zhu decided for us."

"Well, I'm not complaining."

We did our best to make a dent in the feast. We took our time, talking all the while. I got up the nerve to ask her how she supported herself, recalling the pickpocket skills she had demonstrated the first time I met her at the gallery.

"I work when I can," she replied vaguely.

"Where?"

"Here and there."

Wherever "here and there" was, Ninon must have been putting in long hours, because fatigue hung over her like a fog. I told her about my job at the store, and was equally unspecific when I mentioned I did "odd jobs" for a businessman I knew. We had shared our pasts during our picnic on the Islands, but we were still vague about the present. We were like a couple of spies, hiding more than we gave away.

Mama Zhu came by, topped up our teacups, thumped the pot onto the table and said to me, "You change phone now. Remember?"

"Oh, yeah. I mean, no. I forgot."

She held out a small, chubby hand. I fished my Chang phone out of my jeans and gave it to her. From her cardigan pocket she drew a different cell and a slip of paper and plunked them on the table beside my cup.

"New SIM inside. New number on paper," she said, moving off.

"What was all that about?" Ninon inquired, balancing her chopsticks on her rice bowl and dabbing at her perfect mouth with a paper napkin.

"It's a long story."

"So the number you gave me is out of date already."

"That number is for a different phone."

"A diff—?"

"That's a longer story."

She gave me her lopsided smile. "And you say *I'm* mysterious. Anyway, I guess I should go soon."

"Do you have to? No, forget I asked."

"I had a nice time today."

"I wish we could be together more often."

"Maybe—"

"Like, every day."

She stifled a yawn. "Sorry."

A busboy descended on the table and began dumping our dishes into a plastic tub, setting up a racket that made conversation impossible for a few minutes. Then he heaved his burden to his chest, pirouetted, and backed through the swinging doors into a kitchen ringing with the high-pitched voices of people struggling to be heard above the clatter of pots and pans and dishes. As he passed through the doors I had a clear view inside. At the back of the room two women were chatting as they stacked dishes into trays for the automatic washer. One threw back her head and laughed. Turning, she glanced momentarily in my direction just as the door swung shut. White apron, white rubber gloves, white hair net, and a white bandage across her nose.

She was the young woman I'd glimpsed through the curtain at my house.

Ninon was getting to her feet. "I don't see a bill," she said.

"We don't pay," I told her, my eyes still on the kitchen doors.

"We didn't pay last time. How do you manage that?"

"Oh, I did someone a favour once."

Her eyebrows rose but she let it go.

Outside in the street I tried to think of something to say, to keep her with me a few minutes longer. The best I came up with was "So you have to go?"

"I'll see you soon." She patted her satchel. "I've got your number."

"Okay."

She moved closer and put her arms around my waist, resting her head on my chest. I held her against me, her hair soft against my chin, breathing in the odour of her skin and hair. The pedestrians on Spadina flowed around and past us as if we were a rock in a stream. I wanted to stay like that all afternoon.

But Ninon leaned back, kissed me quickly on the mouth, turned and joined the stream of shoppers flowing south. I watched her until she was out of sight.

Back at the house I cleaned up my apartment, then spent the rest of the afternoon mowing and raking the lawn, trimming the edges of the gardens and sweeping out the garage. Putting my tools away, I thought about the face I had seen in the downstairs window a few days before, then today in the restaurant kitchen. When I had cleaned the rooms there had been no evidence of the temporary occupants. There never was.

But now there was a link. I had the sense that some small part of the riddle surrounding Mr. Bai was coming into focus. One of the previous guests was working at the Chongqing Gardens. A coincidence? No. She had only had a quick look at me that morning when I was snooping around outside her window before she flicked the curtain closed, and I was pretty sure she hadn't recognized me when I saw her working the dishwasher in the restaurant.

Assuming the Chongqing Gardens belonged to Mr. Bai—and I didn't know that for a fact—sneaking hired help in and out of the house where I lived was suspicious, not to mention bizarre. If the woman with the bandaged nose was working for him, maybe some or all of the other "guests" were, too. Moving workers in the middle of the night like that strongly suggested something illegal was going on. But what?

They were all Asian. Bai was Chinese. Was he smuggling people into the country to use in his businesses? And if he was, did that explain the stakeout? Were the non-cops really immigration officers of some kind?

"Whoa!" I said out loud. "Slow down, Julian! You're going too fast."

I sat down and went on line, typed "human smuggler" into the search engine, punched Return and sat back. The websites that scrolled onto the screen included news reports, and sites representing governments, women's groups and human rights organizations. I opened a few at random and read the first page of each. It was depressing reading.

The illegal moving of people from one country to another seemed to fall into one of two categories, smuggling and trafficking. The smugglers' human cargo was poor, desperate people. Migrants were promised safe passage to another country where a better life, including jobs and a decent place to live, was waiting—or so they thought. Both the promises made and the fees charged by the smugglers were outrageous. Once the journey—by overcrowded boat, shipping container, a terrifying scramble across unfamiliar terrain in the middle of the night—was over, the smuggler pocketed his fees, disappeared and left the migrants to their fate. Often, people perished on the journey, drowning within sight of their destination or dying of thirst in the back of a truck. Often they were jailed by Immigration as soon as they arrived.

The second group, traffickers, was even more detestable. They seemed to be modern-day slave traders who provided bodies for the sex trade or forced labour. Some victims were even drugged and certain organs were removed and sold on the international black market. Victims of any age and either gender were tricked, kidnapped or hauled away at gunpoint to a fate they could never escape.

I shut down the computer. It made me sick to my stomach to imagine Bai was involved in the kind of thing I was reading about. He couldn't be. It wasn't possible. Maybe I didn't know people very well, but I didn't believe that the soft-spoken man in the office above the restaurant on Spadina trafficked in human beings. Okay, he wasn't in the slave-trader group; that was certain. The smuggler group? I admitted it was possible, but the woman in the restaurant kitchen, chatting away with her workmate, laughing, hadn't seemed exploited to me. I wished I could tell myself that I had no doubts at all.

I put on my gear and went for a long hard run, telling myself the whole time that my imagination was out of control. None of it was my business. My job was to clean the rooms.

Period.

EIGHTEEN

AFTER DINNER SUNDAY NIGHT I fired up the laptop, propped my notebook to the side and began to write a summary of my week's activities for Curtis. It was a report telling him that I had nothing to report. I logged my hours, detailed Marika's movements, included a list of my expenses and e-mailed the statement to him.

I had stacked up a lot of time with nothing to show for it—which was a good thing. Marika's parents wanted Plath to steer clear of her and that was what he had been doing, at least in the afternoons when I was on the case.

The next day, Monday, Marika varied her habitual journey home from the university. When she left the old stone college building she didn't turn left as usual and pass the Soldiers' Tower. Instead, she crossed Hart House Circle and took the few steps down into the Arbor Room café. I hung outside for five minutes before going in, tagging onto a trio of athletic-looking types, then breaking off to get in line for a coffee. The café wasn't busy but there were enough customers scattered around the room to give me cover. I took a table opposite the door, behind Marika and to one side. She sat alone, a cup of steaming liquid and a sticky bun on a paper disc in front of her, a thick textbook open on the table next to her cell. From the side I watched her marking the textbook here and there with a pink highlighter.

I fished a few library books from my backpack and stacked them on my table, opening one at random and pretending to read. There was a quiet, relaxed buzz in the room, low-level conversation, the shuffle of feet, broken by intermittent pings when the woman in the green smock rang up a sale at the food and beverage counter.

It was obvious that Marika was about as interested in her book as I was in mine. She sat quietly, head down, idly turning her untouched drink round and round. Her eyes repeatedly moved from the book to the cell as if she was willing it to ring. She let go of the cup and turned a page, used the highlighter in her other hand, then reached for the cup again.

And knocked it over. The dark liquid raced to the edge of the table and cascaded onto the floor. Too late, she stretched frantically across the table, reaching for the cup. The movement pulled her shirt cuff from her wrist, revealing a vivid bruise on the white skin of her forearm.

She recovered quickly, snatching at her shirt cuff, yanking it into place. She darted to the self-serve area and returned with a wad of napkins, then soaked up the liquid from the floor and table. Her phone rang. She grabbed it and held it to her ear as she carried the sodden napkins to the trash receptacle, then returned and began to pack up her belongings, radiating a sense of urgency.

While she was distracted I gathered my books and left the café before she did, stopping outside on the grass, my back to the door. I slung on my backpack and, taking a guess, ambled in the direction of Queen's Park. Marika hustled past me and turned north. At Bloor Street she crossed with the lights, walking briskly. I followed for ten minutes or so. Then, in the distance, I saw her slip into a movie theatre.

I quickly bought a ticket and entered just in time to see her pull open the door to one of the screening rooms, allowing a surge of music to spill into the lobby. It was the smallest of three theatres, showing a retrospective of Steve McQueen, whoever he was. I lagged a bit to allow Marika to find a seat, then stepped in myself. I stood at the head of the aisle, waiting for my eyes to adjust to the dark while images of a car chase flashed across the screen to the roar of engines and the squeal of tires. There were a few dozen seated patrons scattered in the darkness. I took a seat at the back and scanned the room, taking my time.

Marika was about halfway down, a few seats in from the aisle. Someone was sitting beside her, a tall guy. They kissed, came up for air, kissed again.

It was Jason Plath.

An hour or so later, I stood across the road from the theatre next to a bank machine. A few women gave me suspicious looks as they hurriedly used the ATM. I'm not a robber, I wanted to say to them. I'm an ace private eye, and I just made a big score.

Marika and Plath emerged from the theatre, blinking in the late afternoon light. I was ready for them, snapping photos as fast as the phone camera would repeat. When they kissed goodbye I had them in the frame.

Then they went their separate ways. I went mine.

Seeing a young woman with an ugly welt on her arm necking with the abusive ex-boyfriend who was under a peace bond she had brought against him because of mistreatment was enough to confuse anybody. I wondered if someone would write a song about them someday. Then I tried to put it all out of my mind. It was my job to document Plath if he broke the bond so Curtis could go to the cops, acting for Marika's parents. I had fulfilled the assignment. End of story. But the whole situation certainly was strange.

Rawlins was sitting on the verandah when I got back to the house, his chair tipped back against the wall. He was barefoot, unshaven, his sandy hair rumpled. He held a guitar across his body, his flat pick dancing across the strings, his left hand sliding up and down the neck as his fingers skipped over the frets. In a deep mournful voice he sang a My-baby-done-me-wrong-but-I-love-him-still kind of song. I almost asked him if he knew Marika.

With a final strum he ended the song and said, "Julian. How goes it?"

"Hey, Rawlins. Practicing for a gig tonight?"

"Just whiling away a hot, lazy afternoon. Come on in and have a cool drink."

His kitchen was a tight nook with just enough space for a table and two chairs and a window looking onto the backyard. He pulled a pitcher of iced tea from the fridge and poured two tumblers full. I drank my glass half empty before setting it down.

"Ahhh," I said.

"Been doing thirsty work?"

"I guess so."

Rawlins got to his feet. "Before I forget, I'm gonna be gigging for a while in Kentucky. There's a big bluegrass festival down there. So I'll give you the rent now."

He disappeared into his bedroom. I heard a drawer open and close. He came back with a wad of bills held together with an elastic band. He plunked it beside my glass and sat down.

"Do you like travelling around and performing?" I asked.

"It's a living. It's hard sometimes, with the late nights. Crawling out of bed to get back on the road in time to make the next gig. But it's easier than it used to be. Back in the day I was an awful man for the drink. And sometimes the guys in the band get on my nerves." He laughed. "And vice versa. I've been playing for so many years it's in my blood I suppose."

He took a drink and put down his empty glass.

"Is it lonely sometimes?"

"Oh, yeah, it is that. There are always people around, but when you get right down to it, sometimes you can be lonelier in a crowd than when you're by yourself, if you know what I mean."

"I think I do." I thought again about the song Rawlins had just sung. "You must have met a lot of people over the years."

Rawlins nodded, squinting a bit. He'd caught on that I was headed somewhere.

"Mind if I ask you a question?" I said.

He smiled. "You look dead serious all of a sudden. Go ahead."

"It's about girls—er, women. Do you have much experience with women?"

His mouth twitched, hiding a smile. "Not enough to write a book. I'm not a player, if that's what you mean."

"To be honest, I don't know what I mean. I . . . read this story—I read a lot—about a young woman who goes out with this guy for a while—well, a long time—and he starts treating her bad—a bit like that song you were singing, maybe worse—but she doesn't leave him. Her friends tell her she should, but she makes excuses for him."

Rawlins got up, went to the fridge and retrieved the iced tea. He refilled our glasses and set the pitcher on the table before sitting down again.

"You can't figure out why she stays with him," he said.

"No. Why would she?"

"That question's been around for a long time. I must know a couple of dozen songs on that theme. Bet there's a hundred books about it, too."

"I get it that she loves him," I said. "What I don't get is, how could she? And does he love her? Can you love someone and treat her like crap? None of it makes sense to me."

He chuckled but his laugh had a bitter edge. "What you call sense doesn't have a whole lot to do with it. This, um, story you're talking about. Does the man hit her?"

"Not sure. Maybe. But he's verbally abusive."

Rawlins chuckled again. " 'Verbally abusive.' Sounds a

lot nicer than 'He calls her names, insults her, swears at her, tears her down,' doesn't it?"

"Yeah."

"Well, Julian, here's something you can take to the bank. A man who rips a woman apart with words is a breath away from throwing a punch. As for the woman in your story, I've known—still know—women like that, including my own big sister. They defend the man who mistreats them. 'He didn't mean it. He said he was sorry, he was upset. He's having trouble at work. It's really my fault, I made him angry.' The list of excuses is endless. 'Deep down I know he loves me' is the worst."

Rawlins's face had coloured and his mouth was pinched to a thin line.

"Sorry," I said. "I didn't mean to—"

He recovered quickly. Cleared his throat. "It's a mystery, isn't it?"

"It sure is."

"Well," he drawled, "if you ever find the answer, let me know."

Sleep played hide-and-seek that night, hovering out of reach for a long time. A cool breeze rustled the leaves on the maple behind the garage before slipping through my window screen, a cricket cheeped rhythmically—all sensations that would usually send me off to slumberland in minutes.

But Marika kept me awake, leading my thoughts around in circles. Her behaviour mystified me; maybe that was why, earlier in the evening, I had held back from sending my report along with the supporting photos to Curtis. Plath had thumbed his nose at the peace bond; that should have been the end of it as far as I was concerned. Yet the woman the court had ordered him to avoid had spent over an hour in a theatre with him, romancing in the dark. Then again, Marika seemed like a person with no confidence, with no strength to stand up to Plath. One look at her, with her cowering manner, her way of shrinking inside herself, made her a candidate for intimidation and domination. A guy like Plath could bend her like a green twig.

Yet again, what did I really know about either of them?

I looked at my bedside clock. Three a.m. I told myself I should definitely, as soon as I got up in the morning, write that report.

But that wasn't what I did.

NINETEEN

THE NEXT DAY found me loitering beside a hot-dog cart in front of the Sidney Smith building, where Marika took her class in the history of science. I had swung by Grange Park right after work and hung around as long as I dared without seeing Ninon, then made a dash for the university. The sky had cleared overnight, and the weather had cooled to a pleasant temperature. I tried to ignore the tempting odours of roasting sausage and fried onions as I watched students stream in and out of the building. Spies must have discipline.

Marika appeared. Wearing jeans, a powder-blue silk shirt and leather loafers, she hastened through the front doors with the crowd. When she made the bottom of the stairs I stepped in front of her. With her head down, she almost crashed into me.

"Oh!" she exclaimed.

"Marika Rubashov?" I said, keeping my voice low.

She stopped, looked left and right. "What—who—?" she stammered.

"Sorry to startle you. My name's Paladin. I need to speak with you. It's important."

Before she could reply, I took the initiative. "Is there somewhere quiet we can talk?"

Her eyes squinted with suspicion. "What do you want?"

"I'll explain. Why don't we go to the Arbor Room?"

I hoped if I got her on familiar territory with a lot of people around she might feel less threatened. Her eyes flicked side to side, as if seeking help in the throng of bodies moving around us. She held her backpack against her chest, shoulders pressed inward.

"I'm a friend of Jason's," I lied.

She met my eyes, briefly, then looked down again. "I don't remember him mentioning anyone named—whatever."

"I won't take up much of your time. But we need to talk. Really."

"What about?"

"Let's go to the Arbor Room," I repeated, "and I'll explain."

She relented. Fifteen minutes later we were sitting at a table in the café. I had bought drinks for us. Marika seemed a little less wilted but still wouldn't meet my eyes. She stared at her hands. I took a hit of my coffee and began.

"Okay, here it is. I know about Jason and the peace bond."

Her head snapped up, as if I'd hit her. Her chin dropped. A pink flush bloomed in her face.

"How do—"

"Let me finish. Like I said, I know about the bond. I also know Jason violated it."

"How could you know—whether he did or didn't?" Her dark eyes flashed with anger and her voice rose a notch. "And what business is it?—you're lying—what's going on here?"

"Please keep your voice down."

She reached for her backpack on the chair beside her and planted her hand on the tabletop, moving to get up. But I was holding up my cell, the screen bright with the photo of her and Jason kissing on Bloor Street.

Panic crashed over her. She gasped and dropped back into her seat, shaking.

"Who are you?" she whispered.

"Your parents hired a lawyer to make sure Jason didn't harass you anymore. They didn't trust him to honour the bond. The lawyer hired me."

"And you—what?—*followed* me? Where? For how long? That's sick!"

"Marika, I'm on your side here. I was hired to find out if Jason is bothering you."

"You're the one who's harassing me! Invading my privacy. This is—this is humiliating!"

"If you'll just let me explain—"

Her eyes widened. "I see what you're after. It's blackmail, isn't it? You bastard!"

The whole thing was coming apart. Trying to warn Marika had been a bad idea. I gave it one last shot.

"Think about it for a second, will you? I could have sent the photos to the lawyer yesterday, after I saw you at the theatre. But I held off. I didn't feel right about it. I wanted to talk to you first."

"Yeah, sure, so you could—"

"I don't want anything from you!" I almost shouted, my patience frayed.

She pressed her lips together, red-faced and seething. She took a deep breath.

"Why should I trust you?"

"Because by talking to you I'm putting my job on the line."

She took a drink of cola, her brow creased. "So you know everything."

"Everything? No. I know you met with Jason and spent an hour and a half at the movies with him. I know you were . . . romantic. That's all. I can draw conclusions, make some guesses, but seeing you and him together changed things."

"How?"

"I was hired under a certain understanding, which turns out to be false—maybe. So I have to ask: has Plath ever physically abused you?"

Her eyes dropped and her shoulders slumped. "Never," she said, her voice barely audible. "Sure, we've had fights, but he's never been that way."

Was she lying? Probably. Her instinct would be to protect Plath. Or was it resentment that a stranger had barged into her personal life that made her seem furtive?

"So why did you swear out a peace bond on him?"

This was the ultimate question. The answer would clear up everything, I hoped.

In the same low voice, she replied, "I didn't."

I picked up my mug of coffee and took a slow drink, putting two and two together. If she was telling the truth, her answer shone a bright new light on the whole Rubashov family dynamic.

"Your parents?"

Marika nodded. "I mean, it's true I swore out the bond, but my parents—my father, to be exact—made me."

"But why?"

"Because he hates Jason. He never accepted him. Jason is from the wrong neighbourhood. He only made it to community college. It's the old, tired 'He's not good enough for my daughter' thing. Jason wants me to stand up to my father but I've never been able to. It's pretty much the only thing we argue about.

"One night—I can't believe I'm telling you this—Jason got drunk and came over to the house. He stood under my window, yelling for me to come down and go away with him. He was being an idiot, I know that, but he was upset. My father burst out of the house and confronted him."

"Oh-oh."

"Oh-oh is right. They got into a slanging match, hollering louder and louder. I ran down to the driveway to make them stop. They were standing toe to toe. I screamed at Jason to go home and pushed between them. Jason shoved me aside. I fell. That stopped them both. Jason stood there with his arms hanging down at his sides, bleary-eyed and confused. He was so drunk he could hardly stand up. I finally persuaded him to go home."

Marika picked up her cola and drained it.

"The next day my father said he was going to the police. He made me go with him. I think he was glad, in a way, that he finally had something on Jason. He forced me to tell the cops that Jason had pushed me down—which is assault, he said. And he made me press for a peace bond. It's not fair. Jason didn't mean it."

I felt like I'd heard it all before—because I had. Marika was saying word for word what Rawlins had described.

"Are we done now?" she asked, spitting out the words. "Are you satisfied?"

I didn't reply.

"The next time you go butting into someone's life, maybe you should get your facts straight," she said.

I sighed. "That's what I've been trying to do. That's why I wanted to talk to you."

"Are you going to send the photos to this lawyer my parents went to?"

"I don't know. He was hired by them and he has to answer to them. I'm obliged to report to him. I have to tell him something."

She forced herself to dial back the anger. "Can't you just forget about what you saw? If you tell on us, Jason may be arrested."

"It's possible."

"He'll have a record! It's hard enough to get a job in this city!"

"I'll think about it. That's all I can promise. Maybe you can work this out with your father. Get the bond lifted."

Her eyes flared again. My answer hadn't satisfied her.

"You don't know him. He'd never admit he was wrong. Are you going to keep following me? Because if you do, I'll go to the cops."

"I'm sorry I've upset you. I've got no more to say."

She rose to her feet. Her next words were like acid thrown in my face.

"You know what, Mr. hot-shot investigator? Maybe the peace bond is on the wrong person. Maybe it's my father who deserves it. Or you!"

"Marika, how did you get the bruise on your arm?" I asked.

"You're so smart, you figure it out. Now piss off," she hissed. "This conversation is over."

Then she stomped out of the café.

My old habit of thinking too much was a flaw that complicated simple things, a wind that pushed me off course if I let it. I had humiliated Marika, barged into her life, bullied her into talking about her personal relationships. I had done it to give her a chance, but I hadn't handled it well and I felt bad about the whole scene. What was I going to do? I owed Curtis an accurate report. I had told Marika I'd hold back the photos for a while. Without them, her parents would have nothing solid to take to the cops.

But the ugly welt I had seen on her arm nagged at me. It was the mark left by someone clamping you in his grip until you did what he wanted. Who did it? Plath, or her father?

At home that night I sat down and wrote: *I followed Marika Rubashov to a movie theatre after her afternoon class. Jason Plath was also in the theatre. It was clear that she didn't mind him being there.*

I composed the e-mail and sent it to Curtis.

Without the photos.

TWENTY

THE FOLLOWING DAY I was leaving the store after the morning's work when my Curtis cell rang.

"Want to go to the movies tomorrow?" said the voice on the other end. Suddenly the day brightened.

"Ninon?"

"Surprised?"

"I sure am."

"Well, what do you say?"

"I say yes. Where do we meet?"

"The park. About one o'clock."

"Okay."

"See you."

And she clicked off.

The next morning at work the hours crawled by. My upcoming date was a glimmer of light that I held in the centre of my mind, pushing away the murky questions raised by strange men watching my house, mysterious temporary boarders in the downstairs rooms, and the confusion stirred up by Marika, her ex- or maybe not ex-boyfriend, and her parents. The worst part of the whole three-dimensional mess was that there was nothing I knew for certain, and I felt I was stumbling around blindfolded. Not that the part of my life devoted to Ninon was very clear either.

At last the hands on the clock came around to the position I'd been waiting for. After checking my appearance in the dusty mirror above the sink in the store's cramped bathroom I headed for Grange Park, thoughts of Ninon buzzing like electricity in my veins.

I found her with the two chess players I had talked to weeks before, seated opposite the tall one. She was wearing the same outfit as last time except she'd substituted scuffed, low-cut runners for the sandals. She moved a piece and slapped the plunger on the clock. Her opponent growled.

"Got me again." He looked up at me. "You know this guy?"

In reply Ninon smiled and stood and threw her arms around my neck. She never stopped surprising me.

"Thanks for the game. See you," she said to the two guys, who didn't reply. Hooking her arm in mine, she led me toward Dundas Street.

"So where are we going and what are we about to see?" I asked.

"To the Ryerson University film club's Friday-afternoon screening. They're playing two old French films."

As she spoke she flipped a plasticized card from her pocket.

"See? I'm a member of the film club—for this afternoon anyway," she said, slipping the card back into her pocket.

But not before I noticed the photo on the card wasn't Ninon but a grumpy-looking round-faced guy. I didn't say anything, nor did I point out that I didn't speak French. The prospect of a few hours with Ninon was enough for me.

"I've missed you," I said.

She took my hand but didn't reply.

For the second time that week I found myself on a university campus, but Ryerson's was as different from Marika's school as it could be. There were no stately stone buildings that seemed imported from an earlier century, although our destination, a big three-storey brick structure on Gould Street beside the student union, looked pretty old. We entered and followed hand-lettered signs to the second floor, where double doors had been thrown open to reveal a large room with ranks of chairs arranged before a screen suspended from the ceiling. Most of the chairs were occupied by students, chatting together or thumbing their cells.

"Just walk straight in like you own the whole building," Ninon whispered.

Before I could reply she took my arm and directed me forward. "Hi!" she said cheerily to the guy sitting by the doors and checking IDs. She waved her card in his direction as we sailed by, her thumb covering the owner's image, and we were inside before the doorman could react.

Nice move, I thought.

We found two empty chairs at the back and settled in. I reached over and dragged Ninon's chair toward me until it touched mine.

"I hope you like the films," she whispered. "There are two—*Jean de Florette* and *Manon of the Spring*—spring as in water, not the season."

"I don't speak French, but I can follow the action."

"There are subtitles, I think."

"Oh."

"The best part is, the stories take place in Provence."

I laughed. "I should have known."

The lights dimmed and the screen came to life and the intro credits rolled by to the music of a harmonica. The scenery was beautiful. A grey-white escarpment streaked with pine trees, a stone farmhouse, a stone hovel, stony ground—and cicadas buzzing in the background. Olive groves, vineyards, vegetables—it seemed anything would grow there with enough water. Water was the point of the story, Ninon had told me.

English subtitles began to march across the bottom of the screen like an unstoppable column of soldiers, and I soon tired of switching back and forth between the pictures and the text. The presence of Ninon breathing softly beside me made it hard to concentrate. A young family—parents and a little girl, Manon—moves from the city to a farm. The father is full of dreams and plans, but two locals conspire to make the family fail by blocking up their only source of water—a spring on the nearby mountainside. Crops die.

Sometime during the slow defeat of the family Ninon rested her head on my shoulder, and a bit later I heard her sniffling. Was it the tragic story or seeing her homeland on screen that brought the tears? Or maybe both?

At the end, when her father is dead and her mother sells the farm to the two bad guys, the little girl sees them

unblock the spring. You wonder if she's old enough to realize what has happened, which sets up for the sequel, *Manon
of the Spring*.

The lights came on and the audience scuffled their feet,
yawned, rumbled with quiet conversations. People got up
to walk around or leave the room in search of refreshments.
Ninon sat up and stretched, wiping her eyes with the back
of her hand.

"Good, *non*?" she said.

"Yeah, but sad."

"It's the Garden of Eden story," she replied, adding,
"People can be mean sometimes."

She yawned and stretched again. And that was when I
noticed a red pinpoint on the underside of her arm, just
below the elbow. A needle mark.

My stomach lurched. I stifled a gasp.

"What's the matter?"

"Nothing."

I was on the verge of asking her what caused the mark
when the room lights dimmed and she settled against my
shoulder. The story began to unfold but I was unfocused,
taking in nothing, chasing thoughts around the inside of
my head. I had seen only one puncture wound on Ninon's
arm. Were there more? Not for the first time I was reminded
how little I knew about the girl snuggled up against me,
contentedly taking in the second feature. Homeless people
sometimes turned to drugs to help numb the pain in their
everyday lives. Was Ninon using? Did that explain her pal-
lor and lack of energy at times? Did it account for her
unpredictable behaviour?

I couldn't help myself.

"Ninon," I whispered to the top of her head as it rested on my shoulder.

"Mmm?"

"What's that mark on your arm?"

She looked up, her face almost touching mine. "Tell you later," she whispered.

What could I say? I waited, while Manon took her revenge on the two bad guys and on the townspeople who had kept silent while her family's dreams were ruined.

Ninon and I emerged from the building into the bright afternoon sunlight and made our way to a sidewalk café just around the corner on Bond Street.

"Hungry?" I asked.

"Not right now. You go ahead if you want," she answered.

I was too worried to eat.

"Ninon," I said. "The mark on your arm. Can I ask?"

"Oh, it's nothing. They took a blood sample."

"Because . . ." I let the word hang.

"Because, well, it's a long story."

"I'm not in a hurry."

Ninon sighed. "Well, you don't know this but I sort of live in a kind of hostel. I can stay there three nights running and then I have to leave. But they let me come back. It's just a technicality, they said. As long as I don't stay longer than three nights at a time, I can keep coming there. They're pretty nice."

The Guiding Light Mission.

"And the fourth night?" I asked. "Where do you stay?"

"Here and there. Wherever. Anyway, to get back to my needle mark, which you probably think proves I'm a junkie or something—one of the counsellors at the mission is really nice. Her name's Odetta. She said I was too pale and rundown all the time, so she talked me into letting the hostel's doctor—he comes once a week—take a blood sample. Odetta thinks I might be anemic."

"So a few vitamins and some iron might be all you need."

"Yup." She smiled mischievously. "You look relieved."

I shrugged my shoulders, hoping my guilt didn't show.

"Don't worry about me, Julian. I'm fine."

I cast about for a change in topic. "The movie. Did you recognize the location? I mean, was it filmed near where you grew up?"

"Not real close, no. But the landscape is similar. Seeing the movie reminded me of a million things." Ninon took a long drink. "Do you ever get lonely?"

"Not when I'm with you. But other times? Yeah, but I'm used to it. When you don't really belong anywhere you're never *not* lonely."

"What about those families you stayed with? Didn't they make you feel welcome—at least for a while?"

"They did the best they could. But no matter how hard they tried, I was an outsider. They didn't want me to feel that way, but that was what I was, and I knew it."

Ninon smiled. "It's kind of like fate, isn't it? Us meeting, I mean. Two orphans."

"Thanks to Van Gogh," I said.

"Do you miss your parents? I know you never knew them. Do you miss them anyway?"

I thought for a moment, seeking the right words. "No one has ever asked me that before. The simple answer is yes. It's strange, missing someone you never knew. When I was little I used to imagine who my parents were, what they looked like, what they did for a living, where we lived. I'd give them names. I pictured three people, maybe with a dog, a springer spaniel, sitting in front of the TV watching a sitcom. My mother would bring snacks from the kitchen and we'd munch away, an imaginary family watching an imaginary family on TV. I got in trouble at school sometimes for not paying attention. But how do you explain when the teacher snaps at you, asking why you're not following the lesson, that you were off in dreamland having fun with your made-up parents or playing with your imaginary dog? I haven't daydreamed like that for a long time, though. Too old, I guess."

"I wish things could be the way they used to be," Ninon said sadly.

I took her hand. "Let's be one another's family."

"Someday I'm going back, and I want you to come with me."

"You've got a deal," I replied.

"Promise?"

"Promise."

We sat silently for a while, watching students go to and fro.

"Well, I guess I'd better be on my way," she said.

"Will you let me take you home?"

"No, that's okay. Walk me to the subway?"

"Alright."

On the way there, we made plans to go back to Centre Island Sunday morning. When we reached the entrance to the subway, Ninon stopped and turned to me.

"Bye," she said.

I put my arms around her and kissed her softly. She responded by pressing up against me and prolonging the kiss, and I was carried away by the fragrance of her hair and her skin and the taste of her mouth, like falling through clouds.

TWENTY-ONE

SUNDAY WAS OVERCAST and breezy and showery, but
we took the noon ferry to the island anyway, reversing our
previous route and beginning at Hanlan's Point. We
walked and talked and sometimes laughed, my arm across
Ninon's shoulders, hers around my waist. The air carried
the scent of water and flowers. Ninon seemed to welcome
the times when the drizzle strengthened to rain, forcing us
to take shelter under a tree or a picnic pavilion roof, so she
could rest. The walking seemed to wear her down, but
she insisted on continuing. Near the Centre Island wharf
we stopped at a café.

"You should use the hand-dryer in the washroom to dry
your hair," I suggested.

Shivering, she replied, "Good idea."

I got a couple of big mugs of hot chocolate and took
them to a table. In a few minutes she returned, sat and

reached for her drink. I noticed the inside of her forearm was clear. The needle mark was gone. I didn't ask about the blood test. She'd tell me when she wanted to. She took a sip of the chocolate, swallowed and shivered again.

"That's better," she said. "I'm glad we came, even though the weather is lousy."

We watched a family of mallards waddle through the drizzle to the edge of the lake, then plop in and swim through the rain-dimpled water.

On the return ferry we sat inside the cabin. Ninon looked damp and bedraggled, but happy. At the streetcar stop she kissed me goodbye.

"I'll call you," she said.

"Soon. Okay?"

She nodded and climbed into the waiting streetcar.

That night I got an e-mail from Curtis, short and formal: "Essential that we meet asap. Tomorrow afternoon is best. I'll expect you."

I replied with an affirmative and then sank into a funk. Marika must have gone to her parents after my meeting with her in the Arbor Room and confronted them about hiring a lawyer. I imagined stony words hurled back and forth inside the Rubashov house. Now Curtis would be in trouble with the Rubashovs for breaking a confidence. Marika wasn't supposed to know anything about the surveillance. All of that meant that I was in trouble with Curtis. The whole Rubashov drama was about to crash down on my head.

I sloped through the next morning, my stomach churning

with anxiety, and went directly to Curtis's office as soon as my shift ended. When I opened the door, he was standing at a filing cabinet, his back to me. As if to confirm my doom, he slammed the drawer. He looked over his shoulder.

"Oh, it's you," he said, his voice flat and businesslike.

I didn't reply. I stood by the door, my hand on the knob.

"Better come in and sit down," he said.

I took a chair. I swallowed. Here it comes, I thought. I had made a mistake, acted unwisely. Now it was too late. But I asked myself if I would have done anything differently and the answer was no. So I readied myself to be fired.

He linked his fingers together on the desk blotter. "Something has come up in the Rubashov case," he began, his words clipped and impersonal.

"Look, I'm sorry, but—"

"Sorry? Why?" He smoothed his moustache and goatee with his thumb and forefinger. "How did you know?" he asked.

"Er, know what?"

"What I was going to say."

Something told me to shut up until the fog cleared.

"I misunderstood," I said. "What were you about to tell me?"

He sighed. "That the Rubashov case is beginning to resemble a B movie."

That didn't clear things up. I had no idea what a B movie was.

"The Rubashovs have been, er, approached," Curtis continued.

"Approached . . ."

"By Jason Plath."

"Huh?"

"Exactly. Well put. 'Huh?' indeed. It seems the estimable Mr. Plath has offered to leave town and, more to the point, their daughter."

"Oh."

"For a consideration."

"Meaning a bribe."

"Again, well put."

I had dodged a bullet only to find myself in a funhouse with slanted floors and crazy mirrors. Plath was offering to abandon Marika for money?

"The parents won't agree," I said. "Will they?"

Curtis expelled a puff of air. "They already have."

We were quiet for a moment.

"You did get my report, didn't you?" I asked tentatively.

"Romeo and Juliet at the movies? Yeah."

"And you informed the Rubashovs?"

"Yes, they know. It may well have tipped the balance in favour of accepting Plath's offer. They're going to fork over the money and keep it secret from Marika."

How could they do that to their own daughter? It was clear she loved Plath. Then again, she had no future if Plath was the kind of snake who would take money to leave her, so why not pay him off and get rid of him for good? Maybe they had been right about him all along. But if they felt that way, why not tell her about Plath's demand and prove it? They must have decided she wouldn't believe them.

"Well, that's that, I guess," I said, pulling my notebook

from my pocket. I had decided not to ask for payment if I was getting fired, but now it was different.

"Not quite," Curtis said, preening his moustache once more.

I waited, my book in my hand.

"There's the sticky matter of the consideration. A bank transfer leaves a record, as does a cheque, money order or bank draft. Plath wants cash. A method of payment I support, if it must be done, as I told the clients."

"Uh-huh," I conceded.

"So we need a method of delivery," he pointed out.

"How much are they going to pay him?"

"Many thousands."

"Why not get him to pick it up here? Lawyer-client privilege et cetera."

"Because it's illegal. Technically, it's a form of extortion—you know, like blackmail. I can't get involved. But someone unconnected with this office, acting for the Rubashovs . . ." He let the sentence hang.

"I don't think so. Not this time."

I was firm with Curtis, determined not to let him talk me around the way he usually did, not even when he mentioned a "substantial bonus." I held him off for at least ten minutes. I left the office with instructions on when and where to pick up the cash and where to deliver it.

I almost laughed. I was a character in—what had Curtis called it?—a B movie. I was the delivery boy; the mule; the courier. It was night. No moon or stars. Late. Ten o'clock, to be exact. I entered the lobby of a chain hotel in North

York, walked past the potted ferns and tired sofas to the elevator. Rode to the sixth floor. Walked down the hallway, my trainers whispering on the worn red carpet, looking for room 632. Found it, knocked.

The door opened. In the vestibule, on the floor, stood a mini-duffel bag. Dark blue canvas with fake leather trim. Following Curtis's instructions, I stepped in, picked up the duffel and stepped back into the corridor. The room door closed.

Muttering to myself, I carried the loot down to the street and hailed one of the cabs sitting in the rank by the hotel. I slid into the back seat and gave the driver my destination, Bay and Elm streets.

"I'm on a secret mission," I added. I couldn't help it. The bag full of money was getting to me.

"Really," the cabbie sneered, flicking on the turn signal.

Twenty minutes later the cab pulled to the curb. I paid the fare, collected my receipt and got out. I made sure to adjust my hoodie to cover my head, even though it was a warm, humid night. Gripping the cash-stuffed duffel, I walked west on Elm, leaving the lights and traffic noise of Bay Street behind. Barnaby Place was not much more than an alley linking Elm and Edward streets. My instructions were to walk down the lane until I was contacted. It was silent, unlit, so shadowy I could hardly see my feet as I made my way between two buildings that loomed above me into the dark. A cat screeched. Glass crunched under my shoes. Behind me, something scurried away. I clutched the bag against my chest and kept walking.

About thirty metres farther on, the lane opened up into a sparsely lit parking lot where a solitary tree stood like a sentry among the scattered vehicles. In the distance was the Elm Street bus terminal. Suddenly the location for the drop made sense.

I stopped, checked my watch, straining to see the dial in the gloom.

"Over here," I heard.

The voice, raspy, male, maybe a little nervous, seemed to come from the tree. A shadow separated itself from the trunk—a tall shadow. I walked toward the tree and stopped.

Plath was all business. "Put down the bag and step back."

I did as he said. Eyes on me, he approached, reached down and picked up the duffel. Cradled it in the crook of one arm, unzipped it. Looked inside.

"Hey! What's this!" he exclaimed, slightly tipping the bag so I could see.

I stepped forward, eyes on the jumble of bills barely visible in the gloom. Thunder clapped inside my skull and splinters of light showered before my eyes. I toppled backward, collapsing as the fragments of light flared and died, and felt a stunning crush of pain in the back of my head. I blacked out.

I came to lying flat on my back, my face on fire, my head throbbing. I groaned, rolled over, struggled to my hands and knees, head spinning. I waited until the dizziness faded, then hauled myself to my feet. And vomited.

Coughing and spitting, I stumbled to the taxi rank across the road from the bus terminal, got into a cab and mumbled my address. On the ride home I drifted in and out of consciousness, fighting the nausea racking my guts. An eternity later I pushed through my front door, climbed the stairs, gripping the bannister with both hands, and pounded on Fiona's door.

"God in heaven, Julian! What on earth—?"

"Fiona, I can't see out of my left eye!"

Fiona helped me into her kitchen and I dropped onto a chair. I sat still, half blind, my head spinning. Around me hustled what seemed like three Fionas, clucking and fussing. A tap squeaked, a pan banged, water dribbled. I felt a warm wet cloth on my face.

"Have ye been in a fight, or an accident?" Fiona asked.

"Sucker punch. Clobbered. My eye—"

"Wait a bit," she soothed, gently moving the cloth across my face. "Your eye is swollen shut. That's why you can't see. You've a goose egg high on your cheek, and a wicked abrasion. Here, this will hurt a bit but it'll ease your concern."

I felt fingers prying at my eye.

"I see light!"

"Good." I heard her rummaging around in a drawer. "I'm going to check you for concussion," she said. "Hold still."

The thin ray of illumination played back and forth across my vision.

"Your pupil is dilated. Headache?"

"You're not kidding."

"Nausea?"

"Major."

"Dizziness?"

"On and off. Mostly on."

"You're concussed. That's not good, but you'll live."

Her fingers gently probed my skull, moving slowly through my hair, then she stood behind me.

"Head forward, please. There it is, another goose egg, bleeding. Come on, let's get to the sink."

Fiona was stronger than she looked. She half lifted me out of the chair and guided me to the sink and proceeded to rinse my hair with warm water.

"Men," she muttered, drying my head with a towel that came away with pink stains.

Not long after, head in bandages, a plaster on my cheek, two extra-strength painkillers and a sleeping pill coursing through my veins, I fell asleep on Fiona's couch under one of Roger's blankets.

When I woke up Fiona's apartment was empty. She and Roger had already begun their day. The clock on the stove read eleven. There was a note on the table inviting me to make a cup of tea and ordering me to swallow the pills beside my cup, then spend the day flat on my back.

"You're concussed," the note reminded me, the second word underlined twice. My headache confirmed the message.

But I ignored it. Moving slowly, I washed the pills down with water, folded the blanket and left it on the arm of the couch. Pulling her door hard until the lock clicked, I made my way carefully down the stairs to my own place, still unsteady on my feet. I called the store, explained that I'd had an accident, told Gulun I'd be back on duty as soon as I could, and said goodbye in the middle of his complaint.

Last, my head thudding harder, waiting for the pills to kick in, I sent a "Mission Accomplished" message to Curtis before crawling into my own bed. It didn't take the sleeping pill long to carry me away.

Sometime during the night I heard a car in the driveway and the muffled clunk of the back door opening and closing.

I couldn't have cared less.

I woke up to birdsong and a trickle of sweat crossing my face, stinging my cheek. Bars of afternoon sun shot between the branches of the maple behind the garage and blazed in the window, turning the room into a sauna. I rolled to the edge of the bed and sat up, groggy with heat and the aftereffects of the sleeping pill. A dull ache throbbed in my head, but the dizziness had gone. I got to my feet and padded into the bathroom.

The strange creature in the bathroom mirror, with hair spiking out from under the bandage, looked like a cartoon accident victim. The swollen area under my left eyebrow resembled a slit in the skin of an overripe plum. Plath could throw a punch, for sure.

I stripped off the bandage, wincing when it parted from the cut on the back of my head, and gingerly probed the lump. My fingers came away dry. I stood under the shower for a long while, and by the time I had towelled off, my headache had receded to a faint pulse. I pulled on a shirt and pair of shorts, then took to my chair at the front window, sinking into the upholstery and letting my thoughts run free.

Plath had set up the drop—or the ambush—perfectly. A dark place situated a few dozen metres from the city's main bus terminal. From there, coaches took journeys to all parts of the country and beyond. All he had to do was buy a ticket in advance, time the drop carefully, collect the pay-off, put Julian the delivery boy on the ground to prevent me from following, then saunter across the street and board the bus to who knows where.

Worse than the pain was the prickly humiliation, a burr under my collar. On the ice I had never been a fighter, but I never backed away when an opponent lost control and dropped his gloves, and I was always ready for a sneaky butt-end or elbow to the head. Plath's sucker punch had caught me off guard. I should have been prepared.

I felt like a fool.

TWENTY-TWO

FIONA WAS AT MY DOOR the next morning with Roger balanced on one hip.

"Come on," she said. "I'm on my way to work. We'll drop Roger with Trish and I'll take you into Emerg. You need to have a doctor look at you."

She wouldn't take no for an answer, so I spent an hour in the Emergency department of the hospital where she worked. A doctor—harried, frizzy-haired, with horn-rimmed glasses—pronounced me no longer concussed and added, "I wouldn't enter any beauty contests just yet."

I picked up some painkillers on the way home and added them to my Rubashov expense account. When I pushed open my front door I heard coughing from one of the guest rooms, and the downstairs hall smelled of cigarettes. Back in my apartment I took a couple of the pills and lay down on the couch in front of the TV, dozed off, woke up later, made a coffee and took it to my window chair. I finished a novel and started a new one—a Ken Bruen. I figured no matter how lousy I felt I'd seem bubbling with cheer compared to Bruen's characters.

Later, I made a couple of sandwiches and took them down to the verandah in time to see Rawlins haul three roughed-up instrument cases to the trunk of a cab, on the way to Kentucky and his bluegrass festival. He waved goodbye from the car.

It was a sunny day, with a light breeze rustling around in the giant oak. Even though the verandah was shaded I wore sunglasses. The sunlight hurt my eye. I had missed a couple of days' runs and hoped I'd be able to get back on track tomorrow, but the thought of pounding the pavement with my head the way it was encouraged me to stay put.

Back in my apartment I called Gulun and told him I'd be back to work in the morning.

"I don't pay you for the days you missed," he reminded me before he hung up.

Mrs. Altan's jaw dropped when she saw me next day, and she gaped as if Halloween had come early.

"Julian! What happened?"

I had worked out a story I hoped would explain the puffy, yellowish purple bruise that covered my upper cheek and encircled my eye. I told her I had fallen against the newel post on my stairway at home while I'd been vacuuming the hallway. She looked as if she didn't buy it but didn't pursue the issue.

Gulun surprised me. "You need more time off?" he asked when he came down from his apartment into the back room. "You don't look so good. What—?"

"I'm alright," I said. "Good as new."

Then I told him the tale I had tried on Mrs. Altan. "Hmmph. Newel post with a fist, maybe," he said.

I was up on a ladder resetting the memory of the store's surveillance video camera when Curtis came by. He had on the grey suit today and his clip-on tie was crooked. He looked around and, seeing me, tilted his head toward the coffee machine. I finished with the camera, stowed the ladder in the back room and went to meet him, taking my broom with me. He was stirring pretend-cream into his coffee.

"Here," he whispered, slipping a chubby brown envelope into the pocket of my apron. "That's your expenses and fee from me, along with the, er, bonus from Mr. Rubashov. For services rendered."

"Thanks," I said.

"I think he boosted the fee a little in light of what happened."

"I hope it was all worth it," I replied.

"To you or to the Rubashovs?"

"Them."

"It wasn't."

"How so?"

"Marika has disappeared."

I managed a slow, short—five-kilometre—jog that afternoon. My headache had slowly receded during the morning but the light shock wave of each footfall rippled into my face, agitating the swollen tissue. The envelope Curtis had given me put me in a good mood. For the first time since moving to the house and beginning my job I had earned more than I needed to meet my expenses. I decided to open an account at the nearby credit union and to stash whatever I could whenever I was able.

As I loped down Coxwell to Woodbine Park I thought about Marika—probably the minor pain and irritation in my face brought her to mind. Curtis hadn't sounded all that surprised that she was gone. He probably figured—as I had, as soon as the words left his mouth— that she was with Plath and that they had cooked up the payoff scheme together. I preferred to think that he had planned it and talked her into going along with him. But for all I knew it could have been the other way around. It all came to the same thing. They had extorted money from her parents to make a new start. Before he left the store that morning Curtis had said, "We'll probably see her again."

Meaning Jason would drive her away sooner or later with sharp words or fists, and Marika would shrink back home. But Curtis didn't know that Marika's father was part of the problem. It was more complicated than he thought. That day in the Arbor Room Marika might have been telling me, not in so many words, that the bruise on her arm wasn't the work of Jason Plath but her own parent.

Sometimes I felt sorry for Marika, making her way through the world with her shoulders hunched and her eyes to the ground, pulled in two directions by the men in her life—who should have been there for her. Trying to please one meant angering the other. A classic no-win situation.

I knew what Marika needed.

A river.

PART FOUR

NINON

**Which way does the river run
through this town?
Which way does the wind blow
when the sun goes down?**

—Lennie Gallant

TWENTY-THREE

A WEEK OR SO PASSED.

Ninon and I had a date planned for Friday but she called in the morning and croaked that she wasn't feeling well. Whatever she had sounded bad.

"Where are you?" I asked. "Do you need anything?"

"I'm okay."

"I'm worried about you."

"I'll see you soon."

As if Nature was tuned to my mood, it began to rain, lightly at first, but soon after I arrived at the store the sky opened up, the driven rain bouncing off the pavement and cascading off the window awning. Freshets raced along the gutters, forming tiny lakes at the sewer grates.

I got back home drenched to the skin and kicked off my soaked runners at the top of the stairs, setting them in the boot tray. Inside, I changed, then slipped into a pair of beat-up moccasins and made some sandwiches. I took my plate and a glass of juice to my reading chair. Outside, the rain had faded to a drizzle, and by the time I finished lunch it had stopped altogether.

The house was silent. Rawlins was still away and Fiona was at work—on the day shift this week. I took up my novel and sank deeper into my chair, enjoying the peace. I was into my first Donna Leon mystery. With a different style altogether from the tough-guy detectives who swaggered through the books I usually read, her police detective in Venice, Italy, was more gentle, a deep thinker who didn't seem to work very hard. I read for a while, water droplets pattering on the leaves of the oak tree as it slowly shed what remained of the rain. It was strange how, right after a rainfall, the world seemed to go still, taking a breath before starting up again.

From time to time the prolonged hiss of tires on wet pavement announced a passing car. Then a dark sedan drove slowly around the corner and slipped to the curb down the street from the house. No one got out. I kept on reading, looking up now and again without raising my head, checking on the car. Another watcher.

Maybe my mood had been soured by the disappointment of missing time with Ninon, or by worrying about her, but the idea of some stranger watching my house—again—scraped my nerves raw. I decided to go for a run to settle myself down. I made sure to zip my Chang cell into my backpack. At the front door I pulled down the brim of my baseball cap and stepped outside.

The smell of wet earth floated on the air and the grass glistened with rain. I jogged along the street in the direction of the watcher, studiously ignoring him. A few yards from the sedan I stopped, casually took out the cell, flipped it open and pretended to check the screen, held the phone to my ear. I spoke a few nonsense words, nodded, stole a glance at the car, kept on blathering to nobody. Through the windshield I saw an Asian man in his forties, sporting a white short-sleeved shirt. He sat with his head forward, chin to chest, apparently asleep.

"Where did you go to acting school, buddy?" I said into the mouthpiece. I laughed, nodded again, lowered the cell. Staring at the phone, I faked confusion—hey, what's wrong with this stupid phone?—and pressed buttons hopelessly.

"Damn," I said out loud. I fiddled a bit more, then slapped the cell shut and jammed it into the backpack. But not before I had snapped a few photos. I began to jog, hoping my play-acting was a lot more convincing than the watcher's.

Out of sight, I made sure the photos were clear enough before placing a call to the cut-out. In a few minutes I was talking to Chang.

"There's someone watching the house. A new guy. I haven't seen him before."

"License number?"

I told him, then asked, "Do you want photos?"

"Thank you, Julian, but that won't be necessary." And he clicked off.

I tucked away the cell and ran for two hours. On my way back home I stopped by the motor scooter shop on the Danforth for a few minutes of fantasy. The used 150cc I liked was still on display, a sign shouting "Reduced!!" hanging on the handlebars. They'd have to cut the price a lot more before it fell into my territory.

I jogged slowly for the last few blocks to let my body cool down. I entered the house through the garage and the back door, eavesdropping outside the guest rooms as I passed. No sound. In my apartment I stood under a luke-warm shower for a while, then dressed. I filled a glass of water from the kitchen faucet, gulped it down, refilled it and carried it to the table. When I pulled out a chair to sit on I noticed a tiny dark object, like a bit of pocket fluff, against the lighter material of the seat.

Lowering myself into a different chair, I picked the thing up and put it on the table and pushed it back and forth with my fingertip. It resembled a piece cut from the end of a round boot lace, less than a centimetre long. It was damp, compacted dirt, not fluff. Where had it come from? What had pressed the dirt into such an unusual, tubular shape?

Be logical, I told myself, remembering Occam's razor, a principle of reasoning I had read about in more than one detective story. The idea was that when several solutions to a puzzle seemed possible, the simplest was most likely to be the true one.

So, dirt. Compressed dirt. From damp ground—a gar-den, a field, a bald spot on a lawn. My gardening duties kept me in touch with the condition of the yard. Until today it had been dry. The rain had changed that.

I flicked the bit of dirt around some more, stymied and ready to quit. "I'm just running around in circles," I said out loud.

Running shoes.

The clue was dirt that had been mashed into the tread of a shoe, compressed by the pattern in the sole. But not my sole. The design of my shoes was a mass of overlapping Os.

Besides, I never wore my street shoes in the apartment. I always shucked them onto the boot tray on the landing outside my door.

"Somebody else's," I mumbled the obvious. "But whose?"

The tension in my nerves escalated as I examined the kitchen closely, especially the floor. Finding nothing more, I moved on to the living room, crawling around like a scene-of-crime tech but without the equipment. Almost hidden under my chair lay clue number two—the leather bookmark I had used to flag my place in the Leon novel I was reading before my run. I had left it on the table beside the chair, as I always did.

A close scrutiny of the door to the apartment produced little more in the way of clues—no scratches on the lock or jamb—except a couple of pieces of caked dirt. In my bedroom another bit of earth clung to the fibre of the rug beside my bed.

Back in the kitchen, my Chang cell in my hand, I looked at the chair where I had found the first clue on the seat. The prowler must have stood on it. And the only thing near the table that you'd reach from a chair was the overhead light fixture. Unless the intruder was changing a light bulb for me, I joked to myself, why climb up onto the chair?

The idea of someone creeping around my apartment rattled me. I stopped thinking about it long enough to call the cut-out for the second time that day. When Chang phoned back I got right to the point.

"Someone's been in my apartment," I said, more breathlessly than I wanted to. I gave him the details.

There was a pause.

As cool as I was jittery, Chang said, "Don't say any more. Stay on the line and leave that place."

Outside, I spoke again. "I'm on the verandah."

"Is the car still there—the watcher?"

"No."

"Alright. There are probably eavesdropping devices planted in your apartment, so don't make any more calls from there. Go back inside and turn on the TV and wait."

To pass the time I mulled over a contradiction. The absence of entry marks on my door and the presence of eavesdropping equipment—bugs—suggested a pro. The bits of compressed earth suggested an amateur in a hurry, which was consistent with the fallen bookmark.

It was almost an hour before I heard a car in the driveway and the electric garage door operating. A moment later Chang came into the apartment followed by a thin black man in a windbreaker, toting an aluminum case. When he saw me the always cool Mr. Chang startled, as if looking at a ghost. In the excitement I had forgotten the bruise on my cheek and the black smudge on my eyelid. I was healing but still resembled a boxer who had lost last week's bout. Chang knew nothing about my work for Curtis.

He held his curiosity in check and didn't ask. I was about to tell him the story of the newel post when he shook his head and whispered, "No talking."

The man in the windbreaker stepped over to my TV and pumped the volume even higher. He put his case on the kitchen table, snapped the latches and took out a grey hand-held device about the size of a book, a few pinhead lights and an array of coloured buttons across its surface. He thumbed a button and a light glowed green.

"How many apartments?" he whispered, his voice like a rasp.

"Three. And two single rooms."

"Got keys?"

I took my building superintendent key ring from the hook inside a cupboard door and handed them to him.

"Come back in an hour," he whispered hoarsely.

"Better do the upstairs apartment first," I breathed. "The tenant gets home pretty soon."

He gave me a curt nod. Before we left I took a gander out the window to check the street. All clear. The techie turned up the staircase to Fiona's apartment, and Chang led the way to the garage. His chauffeur, the same one who had driven us to the big restaurant on Spadina long before, was sitting in the dark, erect behind the steering wheel, like an ornament. Chang and I slid into the back seat. My curiosity had me by the throat.

Treading carefully, I asked, "How much am I allowed to know?"

"You needn't concern yourself, Julian. We'll be on our way soon."

To my surprise I found that Chang's icy demeanour didn't intimidate me anymore. I decided to push him.

"That's not really good enough."

He didn't reply. He seemed comfortable with silence.

"Have you thought about the possibility," I went on, "that by keeping me in the dark you increase the chance that I'll make a mistake and say something I shouldn't?"

More silence. Chang looked at his watch.

I wondered how much I should admit to knowing. If I made Chang aware that I had figured out the possible people-smuggling scheme to supply workers for Bai's restaurant—and maybe other businesses—would I put myself in danger of angering Bai to the point that he'd cancel his deal with me, evict me from the house and wipe out my job? Where would I be then?

It's none of your business, I counselled myself for the millionth time. Keep your end of the bargain. At the same time I was irritated by the irony of the whole thing. Bai had provided me with a new identity, a home, a job, out of what Chang had insisted was a deep sense of appreciation. Bai was indebted to me. Why then was I completely dependent on him? Shouldn't I be the one dictating the terms?

I tried another tack.

"Look," I began as calmly as I could. "If the police get involved in whatever is going on here I might be discovered and lose everything I have. Okay, it's a slim chance. But it makes me nervous. Somebody broke into my apartment—probably a professional—the door wasn't forced. That technician you brought along is going to find bugs in the rooms you're using to move people around. Whose bugs are they? Do you know? Can you tell me?"

Chang's face was as blank as a brick wall.

"We know," he replied.

And that was all he said.

The techie, whose name I hadn't been told, came through the door and got into the car beside the driver. In all, he had discovered eight listening devices. Top of the line, he told Chang. Rawlins, my place, the two downstairs rooms. Only Fiona's place was clean.

"That concludes today's work," Chang announced. "We'll need to sweep the house regularly from now on. Good day, Julian, and thank you."

I climbed out of the car and the chauffeur backed out the driveway and motored away.

Had cops planted the bugs? Or immigration officials? Both were possible actors in the drama, but professionals, either cop or government, weren't consistent with the watchers. Those guys were amateurs.

And they were all Asian. And Chang and company were Asian.

Then again, the techie Chang had brought along wasn't.

The pieces didn't fit together no matter how I moved them around.

"Although . . . ," I mused as, back in my apartment, I poured tea into a mug and sat down at the table, under the light that until a few minutes ago had held a listening device.

Police forces, no matter what their category, weren't the only people who used high-tech surveillance. You could buy all kinds of "spy" toys at any electronics store. Everybody knew that. I cast my thoughts wider, keeping in mind Occam's razor.

Then, inspiration. "You blockhead," I hissed with disgust. How could I have missed it?

Fact one: I got involved with Bai because of a kidnap attempt. The men who tried to grab the obnoxious little Wesley were crooks. Asian crooks.

In meeting my request for a new identity, Bai had had to break a few laws, even if his offences weren't as threatening as kidnapping or breaking and entering.

Bai and Chang seemed to be involved in illegal activity having to do with immigration.

Was it like a TV show? Was it really that simple? A conflict between rival criminal organizations?

And was I right in the middle of the whole mess?

TWENTY-FOUR

"WHAT HAPPENED?" Ninon gasped, her eyes wide with surprise, when she met me at the streetcar stop. We hadn't been together since before the Rubashov case wound up.

"Aw, a guy caught me off guard."

"But why?"

"A minor disagreement. Not important."

As soon as I said the words I wished I could take them back. Being secretive had been an automatic response for so long I'd forgotten how to talk normally. My answer was a reflex. I realized I wanted to tell her, to share more of myself.

So I did. As the streetcar carried us toward High Park I told her about the work I'd been doing for Curtis on the Marika case, including Plath rearranging my face and Fiona helping me. I was rewarded with the ironic smile.

"I didn't know my boyfriend was a private eye," she joked.

"Hey, it's a living."

At High Park we walked to the grassy slopes beside Grenadier Pond. It was a perfect day, the clear sky a blue dome above, the breeze off the lake soft and cool, the beds of flowers a riot of colour against the green lawns. Ninon, in her T-shirt and shorts and leather sandals, looked summery and beautiful. Very kissable. But her flu was making her suffer with puffy eyes and cheeks glowing with fever. Periodically, coughs shook from deep in her chest. I should have postponed the picnic.

We spread our blanket beside a flower bed with a view of the pond and unwrapped the sandwiches. Ninon tried to eat, but each bout of coughing seemed to tear something loose inside her. She rummaged in her backpack and came up with a bottle of cough syrup. That helped a bit. I ate sandwiches guiltily while we talked, but Ninon had no appetite.

"Do you mind if I ask you something?" I said.

"How can I say if I'd mind until I hear the question?"

"So . . ."

"So ask."

"I've always wondered why you didn't want me to know where you live. You said it's a hostel, but that's all."

Ninon looked away, as if something on the far shore of the pond had suddenly attracted her attention. I waited. Finally she replied.

"I never told you because I'm ashamed."

A second later there were tears rolling down her cheeks.

"I'm sorry," I murmured. "I shouldn't have—"

"It used to be that I lived in a big sunny flat with my parents and I had my own room with a view over the *quai* to the big school across the way. My *maman* was a respected seamstress with her own business. My *papa* was a chef. Now they're dead and I'm in a foreign country and I'm poor—no, not poor. Destitute. I live in a mission, sleep in a dorm with other women. I beg on street corners. And I *steal!*"

That word released a flood of emotion she had held back for a long time. I pushed her satchel aside and put my arm around her. After a while she calmed. I knelt in front of her and wiped away her tears with my shirt-tail.

"Not very romantic," I said. "I should have brought a hanky."

I wanted to ask Ninon to move into my apartment. There was lots of room. She'd be off the streets and she could look for work in the neighbourhood. But I couldn't say anything or raise her hopes until I was sure. Lately my place wasn't safe, and it wouldn't be until whatever was going on stopped going on. And when would that be?

Her eyes, still pooled with tears, were so sorrowful I felt my throat swell.

"Julian," she whispered. "You're the only one who cares about me."

I felt water gather in my own eyes. She scrambled to her knees and put her arms around me and we held each other.

"I love you," I said.

She squeezed me tighter. "Me too."

"Things will get better," I soothed. "We can work together. You're not alone anymore."

Then Ninon whispered in the playful voice I wished I could hear more often, "You and me. Team Orphan."

I laughed. "Team Orphan."

It seemed a good time to kiss, so we did.

"You'll catch my cold," she said, coughing.

We lay back on the blanket, holding hands and talking, shielding our eyes from the blue intensity above us. The "here and there" job Ninon had pretended to have turned out to be begging. I couldn't criticize. It was what you did when you ran out of choices. Maybe I could ask Bai if he could find her a job. But it seemed the wrong time to approach him, when I was up in the air about him. For all I knew I could be on my own too, soon. I might be a step away from begging myself.

We walked around the park a bit, but as time passed, Ninon's flu seemed to get worse.

"You should go to a clinic," I suggested.

"I'll shake it off in a few days."

"St. Joseph's hospital is nearby. We could go there."

She shook her head.

"What did the doctor say?"

Confused, she asked, "What doctor?"

"The one at the, er, place you stay. He took some blood?"

Ninon was made breathless by a coughing fit. When it cleared she said, "I didn't hear anything. I think he forgot about me."

"Well, you ought to follow up on that. I'm worried about you. You should be in bed. Let's go."

On the way back, the swaying of the streetcar lulled Ninon to sleep. I didn't wake her until we got to the stop near the mission. I helped her down the streetcar's steps and put my arm around her.

"I'll be okay now," she said.

She didn't want me to walk with her to the mission, even though I could see the white sign from there.

"Alright. Call me if you need anything."

Slipping her satchel strap over her shoulder, she nodded.

"Promise," I said.

Ninon smiled. "Promise."

She walked down the deserted street, her head down, her slender back bent slightly to take the weight of her carryall. When she disappeared into the building I turned and, deciding to go part of the way home on foot, headed north, strolling along by myself toward an empty apartment, wondering if I looked as lost as Ninon did.

TWENTY-FIVE

WHEN I GOT TO MY STREET I noticed the watcher right away.

I stopped and stared at the car. After my short break with Ninon the mysteries rushed back, taunting me, telling me I was just a bystander in a game whose rules I couldn't even figure out, much less follow. Suddenly I was fed up. What was the point of making a new life for myself when I was allowing it to be ruined even before it got properly underway? I wasn't the painter anymore; I was the canvas.

I turned onto my footpath as usual, but I dropped my pack on the verandah and grabbed the folded lawn chair that was leaning against the railing. Whether it was fuelled by worry over Ninon's worsening health or frustration with the irritating state of ignorance I constantly found myself in, a rush of adrenaline propelled me down the road. Eyes glued to the watcher's windshield, I banged the chair onto the sidewalk directly across the street from him, sat down and stared at him through the car window.

He glanced my way, then snapped his head back around, eyes front, pretending not to notice me. I kept my eyes on him, my breathing fast and shallow, my blood boiling. He fished a road map out of his glove compartment, unfolded it and pretended to consult it as if it held directions to buried treasure. His incompetence only goaded my anger.

While he studied his map I got up and circled the car, stopping a few paces in front of the hood. I pulled out my cell and took a photo of the license plate and a few pictures of the watcher. That seemed to rattle him. I returned to my chair and resumed staring. Eventually he folded his map, started the car and drove sedately up the street. What a clown!

The whole episode had lasted no more than a few minutes. When I got back to my apartment, my hands were shaking.

As if things weren't confusing enough, a new guest arrived that night. He was no underfed, scared young woman destined for a restaurant kitchen. He was confident enough to break the most sacred of Chang's rules, leaving his room the next morning to knock on my door just as I was getting ready to go to work. Dressed in a rumpled blue three-piece, stocky, with wire-framed glasses perched on a broad fleshy nose, he looked like some kind of professional who had seen better days. He also stank of cigarette smoke.

"I from downstairs," he announced in broken English.

"Oh," I replied, shocked to see him out of his room. None of the other guests had voluntarily shown their faces. It was strictly against Chang's regulations.

"Er, come in."

He took a step inside the apartment, his face pinched with anxiety. A man out of his element.

"They not to give me *xiang yan*."

"Oh," I said again.

"Cigarette," he explained, holding up his hand and forming a V with the first two fingers. "You have?"

I shook my head. "But I can bring you some, I guess. I work in a store."

Behind the glasses his eyes slid to the side as he processed the words.

"Thank-a-you. Now?"

"No, I can't. After lunch."

"Mmm, long time."

Where did he get off, being so demanding?

"Best I can do."

The man nodded and left, thumping not at all secretively down the stairs. A moment later I heard his door open and close. I locked up and headed off to work.

Soon after I got home, a cough told me the smoker was back on my doorstep.

He followed me into the kitchen, where I had begun to make lunch—a few samosas heated up in the micro and a pot of tea. He eyed my backpack, scratching his ear with nicotine-stained fingers. I plugged in the kettle, then pulled out two packs of "tax-free"—smuggled—cigarettes and put them on the table.

"Here you are."

He picked up one pack and broke the seal. I stopped him.

"Sorry, no. Not in here. Outside or in your room."

I handed him the second pack.

"Come back and have some tea."

"Yes, yes. I will back. Thank-a-you."

Half an hour later we were sitting at the table, crumb-strewn plates and a second mug of tea before us, stumbling through a halting conversation about not very much. He never gave me his name and I didn't ask. More Chang-inspired hush-hush. I wondered what had brought him to this country. He was different from the others, who were, from what I could tell, anonymous and frightened. This man was uneasy—I could see that in his face and gestures—but underneath were signs of confidence. He was apparently not interested in spending all of his time under a blanket in his room.

"I sorry my poor English," he said. "I am, mmm, rusty. That is the word?"

"Yeah. It'll do."

For the first time he seemed to relax a bit. He sat back and looked around the kitchen and living room. "You have many books," he observed, looking at the full shelf in the living room.

"Would you like to borrow a few?"

The next thing I knew he was on his knees, pulling paperbacks from the shelf.

"No offence, but can you read them alright?"

"Yes, yes," he replied. "I read well. Speaking very . . ."

"Rusty."

"*Dui!* Yes."

He got to his feet, smiling, clutching a half-dozen mysteries. He had nothing to do in his room all day except smoke and wait and worry until Chang sent someone to whisk him away some night. There was no TV or radio in either downstairs room. The boredom must be driving him nuts.

"Would you like me to bring you a newspaper?" I asked.

"You can get English? Chinese?"

"I'll try."

I could ask Mama Zhu what Chinese papers to buy.

"Can you tell me your name?" I asked on impulse, thinking maybe he'd break this rule too.

"*Lao* Chang say not."

"Well then, what should I call you?"

His eyes rolled up as he thought. "I choose an English name . . . um, Charr."

This is an English name? "Did you say Charr?"

"Yes. You know Charr Dicken? Famous English writer? I very like his books. I borrow his name."

"Okay, Charr it is. I'm Julian."

He nodded. "Jurian."

"Close enough," I said.

After Charr had thumped back down to his room with his books, I looked up the number of the mission and, perched on the edge of my window chair with my eye on the street outside, punched the number into my work cell.

"Guiding Light."

A male voice, ageless and uninviting.

"I'd like to speak to Ninon Bisset if she's there."

"Staff only."

"Pardon me?"

"You can only talk to someone on our staff. We don't give out the name of anyone who may or may not be a guest at the mission."

"But she's a regular. If you could just tell her—"

"And we certainly don't take messages."

"Will you at least let me know—"

"Have a nice day."

And he ended the call.

I stabbed the OFF button on the cell. I hadn't really expected to be able to talk to Ninon, but I was hoping. Should I go over there? I wondered. I probably wouldn't get past the doorbell. Some of the people who made use of the mission would be, like Ninon and me, on the run— hiding—and regardless, as the man had grumpily told me, the mission wasn't there to act as a message service. But images of Ninon shuddering from a coughing fit and burning up with fever wouldn't leave me alone. I pulled on my running togs and, although the mission was a long way off, I included it in my route for the day.

No luck. She may have been there. Or on the moon, for all I was able to discover. I jogged off, wishing she'd call and let me know how she was doing.

After supper I was out front, cultivating the flower beds that skirted the verandah, when a cab deposited Rawlins and his travel bag and four instrument cases on the sidewalk. I wiped the sweat off my forehead, propped the cultivator against the porch railing and went to help him with his baggage.

"You have an extra guitar," I said in greeting, picking up two of the cases.

Despite the heat, Rawlins was sporting a long-sleeved, snap-button shirt with pointy pocket flaps, faded denims and dusty cowboy boots.

"Hey, Julian. Yeah, bought the new one in Kentucky. Come on in and take a look."

A few minutes later, after throwing open every window in his stuffy apartment, Rawlins flipped the latches on the case and, with a wide grin on his weathered face, held up the instrument for my inspection. It was a six-string, all black, polished smooth as glass, with gold tuning pegs and an inlaid pearl Q on the head.

"Wow."

"Brand new. Handmade. Ordered it two years ago from the artisan; he's a slow worker but worth the wait. Solid top, sides and back—the guitar, not the craftsman. Want to hear it?"

"Yeah."

While Rawlins tuned the guitar I pushed aside a stack of sheet music and sat on the couch looking around, wondering where Chang's techie had discovered the bugs— something I wouldn't be telling Rawlins about. He began to play, using a flat pick and his fingers. A piece he called "The Drummers of England" flowed out of the instrument, the beat steady and brisk, but not military or aggressive like the title suggested. I wished I knew something about music. The tune was beautiful. I liked it, but I didn't know why I liked it. I wondered how long it took to be as good as Rawlins.

When he finished, I asked, "Did you make up the tune?"

"Wish I had. No, that's a Barenberg piece."

"Well, the new guitar sounds fantastic."

As if he'd tuned in on my thinking, Rawlins added, "You know, Julian, I could have you making music—not concert grade, but a beginning—in a month, if you want."

I was tempted, but with all the confusion in my life right then, I couldn't see my way clear.

"Maybe one of these days," I replied.

As the dark came on, the breeze dropped, leaving the air velvety and close. Sitting in my chair by the window, I heard guitar music downstairs. I could also detect cigarette smoke floating on the sultry air coming through my window screen. I guessed that Charr was on the verandah. He wasn't even supposed to be out of his room, never mind outside the house.

I found him sitting on a lawn chair, eyes closed, head back, a cigarette burning between his fingers. Enjoying the music, I supposed. Who could blame him? His room would be roasting, the air stiff and stale. The clap of the screen door as I came out broke his reverie.

"Ah, Jurian. Thank you for newspaper."

I had popped into a shop near home at the end of my run and picked up a couple of dailies for him.

"That's okay," I replied, sitting on the verandah swing. "Hey, I never asked. Do you have enough food?"

"Chang give me."

I nodded. Maybe it was the peaceful night, the mood created by the music, but I thought Charr might open up a little.

"You come from China," I began.

Charr nodded. I waited but nothing more came.

"What part of China?" I asked, as if his reply would make a dent in my total ignorance of the place.

He tapped another smoke from the almost empty pack and lit up.

"North part," he replied vaguely.

Okay, he wouldn't play. Might as well go for broke.

"I guess Mr. Bai helped you get to this country," I said casually, studying his face.

He tried not to show a reaction, but, behind his glasses his eyes narrowed for a split second.

"I not know this person."

I gave up and changed the subject. "It sure is a nice night."

He restricted himself to a nod.

We sat back and let Rawlins's guitar serenade us with a slow ballad. I recognized the tune but couldn't name it. I let my mind float with the music, wondering what Charr's story was. It couldn't have been easy, uprooting his life, leaving home, wherever that was, and sneaking into a strange country, almost certainly illegally. You didn't have to be an outlaw to understand that wrenching yourself away from everything familiar and trying to find a footing in an alien place was harder than people thought. Ninon hadn't managed it. Not really. I wasn't sure I had either—even though I'd had lots of practice, and I had been born here.

Thinking about Ninon got me worrying again. I wished she'd call. I wished I could think of a way she could get out of the dead-end life she was in.

Out on the street a car rolled slowly by.

Too slowly.

It drifted past the house, the purr of the engine hanging in the still air. A black car. Two Asian men inside, the one riding shotgun boldly studying us through his open window.

As nonchalantly as I could I told Charr, "I think we'd better go inside."

TWENTY-SIX

THE NEXT DAY WAS HOT, and the thick air stalled over the city was heavy with moisture. I came straight home from work, a couple of newspapers for Charr tucked under my arm, their pages limp with humidity. I had promised Fiona that morning that I'd babysit Roger for an hour while Trish took her own kid to the doctor. When I turned the corner onto my street I dropped the papers and began to run.

There was a car parked in front of the house, and two guys in suits on the verandah. One of them had his hand on the doorknob. I dashed up the path and onto the porch, startling the strangers. They were the men who had cased the house last night.

They could have been twins—medium height, beige lightweight suits, slicked-back hair, dark eyes with an irritated, menacing air—but one was smooth-skinned, the other pockmarked high on his cheeks.

"What can I do for you?" I asked, not very politely.

The one who rode shotgun in the car the night before replied in a calm, bureaucratic tone, "We are looking for a friend."

"What's his name?"

The man offered a cold smile. "We don't want to trouble you." He said something in Chinese and his partner rapped loudly on the door.

"There's a few people living here, including me," I told him, keeping my voice even. "Who do you want to see?"

The partner knocked again.

"Look," I tried again. "I'm the building superintendent. You'll have to give me a name."

"A friend," repeated the bureaucrat.

"Excuse me," I muttered to the knocker, pushing between him and the door, forcing him to take a step back. He threw a what-do-you-want-me-to-do glance to the bureaucrat, who gave an almost unnoticeable shake of his head.

"I think you'd better leave," I said.

Neither man made a move, the bureaucrat hiding behind a polite mask, the knocker standing with balled fists. I pulled out my cell.

"You're trespassing. Go now, or I'll call 911."

They stared at me a moment longer, and when I didn't back down the bureaucrat snapped off a few words in his native language, turned and walked down the steps, his silent partner behind him. They got back into the car and drove off. I caught their license plate on the cell camera, although Chang wouldn't need it, I was sure.

I had no time to think about what had happened. I was due at Fiona's in two minutes. I knocked on Charr's door and told him he shouldn't come out of his room today. He didn't argue. I dashed up the stairs to find Fiona waiting, in a hurry as always. But she took time to cup my chin in her hand and turn my head from side to side, peering at my eye as if she expected it to fall out.

"Coming along nicely," she pronounced. "The lassies'll be chasing you again in no time. Roger's sleeping, but he'll likely wake soon. You know where I keep the diapers. His milk's in the fridge. Bye, Julian, and thanks."

And she was out the door, her feet drumming on the stairs, the screen door slapping in her wake.

The superheated apartment was in a state of semi-organized confusion. I sat down on the couch, still pumped by my adventure with the two beige suits. Later, Trish arrived at the door—which I had propped open to let some of the stifling air escape—to find me and Roger on the floor in front of the TV, putting an oversized jungle animal jig-saw puzzle together for the sixth time.

"If you're free for the rest of your life, I know a few young mothers who'd snap you up in a second," she purred over the head of the baby she held against her chest.

I carried Roger downstairs and lowered him into his stroller and Trish set off down the sidewalk, skilfully pilot-ing one stroller with each hand. I watched them go, then called Chang.

I was late getting to bed that night and sleep wouldn't come. Not even a breath of air flowed over the window-sill. Things were piling up. Ninon was constantly at the centre of my thoughts. The situation with Charr—the whole Chang thing—was spinning out of control. I felt like I'd been blindfolded and tied to a violent amusement park ride.

I got up and drew a glass of water from the kitchen faucet and drank it by the back window. Mist haloed the street light and softened the outlines of the cars along the curb.

I heard voices, urgent but controlled, from the downstairs hall.

Barefoot, wearing only my boxers, I threw open my door and dashed down the stairs, swung round the newel post and landed in the hall on both feet. The suits I had kicked off the verandah that afternoon were at Charr's door, talking rapidly in low tones. Charr, in trousers and a greyed tank top, gripping one of my paperbacks in his hand, was shaking his head and yelling, "*Bu xing! Zou kai! Zou kai!*" at the man who held him fast by the opposite wrist.

But the pockmarked man held on.

"Hey!" I hollered. "Let him be!"

The bureaucrat rattled off a sentence or two and his partner let Charr go. Both suits turned to face me, and at that moment Charr seized his chance, ducking back into his apartment and slamming the door and throwing the bolt, leaving me alone to face the suits.

I stood blocking the hallway, aware of how ridiculous I must look in my red plaid boxers.

"Who are you?" I demanded.

The bureaucrat did the talking. "This is not your business," he said, as if quietly addressing an employee, his arrogance rising from him like a sharp odour. "I advise you to—"

"You stand here in *my* house," I hissed, "and tell me this is none of my business? You come here and give *me* advice? I asked you who you are."

"We will go now," the bureaucrat insisted. But he didn't move.

The partner's body language was subtle, but he was preparing to do something. I kept my eyes on his and stood my ground.

Stalemate.

"We will go now," the bureaucrat repeated. "Please move aside."

Whether his forced smoothness was meant to calm me or his partner I couldn't tell. Deciding I could gain nothing by obstructing them, I opened the front door wide, faking politeness, Mr. Good Host seeing off his honoured guests. The bureaucrat glided past me. His flunky kept up the staring contest, wary, expecting a move from me. I almost laughed when he pirouetted and backed out of the house, eyes locked on mine, like a gunslinger in an old Western withdrawing from a hostile saloon crowd.

And then they were gone.

I rested my hand on the staircase railing, felt the rivulets of sweat trickle over my ribs, the tremor in my hands. I didn't feel like discussing the incident with Charr—not tonight, anyway—so I padded up the stairs. I drank a glass of water, then picked up the Chang cell. After I made my report he said he'd be along as soon as he could.

I wished everything was as simple as Roger's jigsaw puzzle, with its happy lion cavorting in the grassland with a giraffe and a rhino. Tonight I had been up against pros. The main door to the house was locked every night. The suits had gotten in anyway without making a sound. Were they the ones who had planted the bugs? Or had they had it done? I couldn't picture Mr. Bureaucrat doing anything that might wrinkle his suit or get his hands dusty. Who were they, he and his pockmarked partner?

My rival-gang theory, connecting the abduction attempt on Wesley with Mr. Bai's wealth and resources and apparently illegal activities, was weakened by tonight's events. When I blocked Wesley's kidnappers, one of the men had come at me with a knife. Tonight was different. Although the bureaucrat's partner oozed aggression, suggesting he could break loose and have you on your back before you knew what hit you, he and his boss were restrained. They were all business. They operated within limits. It would have been easy to pop Charr on the head, drag him to the car and make off with him. Instead, they'd tried hard to persuade him to co-operate. When the bureaucrat had noticed his sidekick had Charr by the arm, he had ordered him to lay off.

I also found it hard to believe the suits were part of the amateur-hour watchers group. Still, nothing fit. There was only one person who could connect the dots for me.

His car pulled into the driveway thirty minutes later.

TWENTY-SEVEN

As it turned out, two cars rolled up to the garage—identical models, each driven by a chauffeur in a peaked cap.

When Chang came into the apartment he found his ward at my kitchen table holding a mug of tea in a trembling hand. Chang shook hands with him, firing off a few questions in Chinese as he pulled up a chair for himself. He sounded respectful, not as smooth as he had been with Mr. Bai on my visit to Bai's office above the restaurant, but close. Charr, his chin quivering, replied at length, nodding in my direction a few times.

Chang turned to me. "It is imperative that we move our guest immediately. I arranged the cars as quickly as I could. He will be in one of them, out of sight. The other is a decoy."

"Which gives the bad guys a fifty-fifty chance of picking the right one and following it," I countered. "That's if they have only one vehicle. If they have two, your plan collapses."

Chang nodded. "I have thought of that but I was only able to—"

"There's another way."

I must admit I enjoyed seeing his eyebrows rise, silently asking me what I had in mind.

So I told him.

Then I turned off the light.

It took only a few minutes to go downstairs and help Charr gather his possessions—a few articles of clothing, which he jammed into a small suitcase together with his remaining cigarettes and two of the novels he had borrowed but hadn't read yet. As we left his room I switched his light off.

"No, this way," I said when he turned toward the door to the garage. "Back upstairs."

He and I sat together in my darkened kitchen, Charr clutching the handle of the suitcase resting on his knees. Below, I heard car doors open and close. I went to the window, keeping out of sight as I peered around the frame. The sedans, one after the other, reversed into the road and sped away in opposite directions. In one of them, Chang would be crouching out of sight behind the front seats. The other car would have no passenger.

The plan was for Charr and me to wait half an hour. I felt sorry for him, not knowing where he was bound, forced to trust a stranger less than half his age. Then he did something that showed me he was a survivor no matter how scared he was. He opened the suitcase and took out a pack of smokes and a well-worn deck of cards secured with an elastic band. He held the cigarettes up.

"*Ke yi ma?* I may?"

"Just this once."

He smiled and lit up. "I teach you Chinese game."

"Okay."

I hate card games, but anything was better than sitting anxiously in the dark watching a scared fugitive chain-smoke. The game was like blackjack, or twenty-one, but the object was to take turns slapping down cards, counting up the accumulating value in your head and blurting out the total before the other guy did. In the unlit room we read the cards as best we could and whispered the points totals.

When the time came I picked up my cell, keyed in the number I had looked up earlier, gave some instructions and ended the call.

"Let's go," I said.

Charr snapped the elastic around his cards and stowed them, checked the suitcase latches, got up and ran his cigarette under the faucet. I led the way downstairs and through the garage and out the pedestrian door, first checking for movement on the misty street. The humidity muffled city night noises, even a siren wailing in the distance. The plan was to make use of the unlit lane that ran behind the yards on my street. The lane had been put in years before, when the neighbourhood was built, to provide access to the detached garages behind the houses. Charr and I would head south, crossing four or five yards, then cut out into the lane.

We set out, and soon ran into our first problem—a fence that I knew about but hadn't realized would be such a challenge for a not very tall, middle-aged fugitive.

"Wait till I'm across, then give me the suitcase and follow me," I whispered.

I vaulted the wooden barrier. Charr handed the case over and attempted to haul himself up and over, got high enough to balance on his chest. He grunted and puffed as his shoes scrabbled on the boards.

"Wait," I said, hopping back across.

I made a footrest by interlacing my fingers. Charr got the idea and made it to the top, teetered awkwardly, then dropped like a sack of bricks to the other side.

"Oof!" he said.

"Shhh!"

I found him crouching on all fours in a flower bed. A dog barked. Then another. We froze. Charr, wide-eyed, looked about.

"I afraid dogs," he whispered.

"Don't worry, they're not close," I assured him. "Let's go."

Four more fences and a sprained ankle later, we sneaked down a driveway between two houses and came out onto the lane, Charr limping and clutching my arm. I toted his suitcase, flashing back to my escape with Wesley. We made it to the intersection of a side street and the lane, where a taxi was waiting, lights out, engine off.

I pulled open the rear door.

"You're late," the cabbie grumbled. "I was gettin' ready to pull out."

I helped Charr into the cab and laid the little suitcase on his lap. He gripped it as if it was a lifebelt.

"You have the destination, right?" I asked the driver, handing some bills across the seat to him.

"Yep."

I patted Charr on the shoulder, and he grabbed my hand and squeezed it before letting go.

I checked with the cabbie. "The directions are clear?"

"As a bell. What is this guy, a spy or somethin'?"

Watching the cab start up and pull away I muttered, "I wish I knew."

I killed an hour and a half watching a late-night movie, drumming my fingers on my thigh, before I phoned the cut-out. I'd never seen Chang show any kind of mood, emotion or fatigue—but when he replied, he sounded weary.

"Yes, Julian."

"I just wanted to be sure that Charr—that the guest made it safely."

"He did."

I waited for more, but it didn't come.

"You weren't going to let me know, were you? *I* had to call *you*."

"Everything has been taken care of."

"I was worried about him."

"You needn't concern yourself, Julian. But thank you for your help," he said stiffly.

A hot flush bloomed in my neck and face. Not concern myself? I had no idea what was happening right where I lived. I could be in danger—from cops or spies or crooks, I didn't know. The so-called guests—especially Charr—could be under threat. And the guy with the answers apparently didn't think I deserved any kind of explanation.

Chang's offhand, phony politeness stuck like a bone in my throat.

Be the painter, I told myself.

"Was there something else, Julian?"

"I want a meeting with Mr. Bai," I blurted.

Pause.

"Mr. Bai is quite busy these days. Perhaps—"

"No, Mr. Chang," I cut in. "No 'perhaps.' Definitely. You are my contact with Mr. Bai and I'm telling you I want a meeting with him."

I heard a great sigh at the other end. Or did Chang's second-long pause cause me to imagine it?

"All right, Julian, I'll do my best."

Another brush-off.

"If I don't hear back from you in, let's say, two days, I'll come over to Mr. Bai's office myself. And I won't leave until I see him."

This time *I* cut the connection.

As soon as I put down my cell I began to second-guess what I'd done. If I pushed Mr. Bai he might get angry. This might not be my home anymore. I might have to leave my job. I'd lose the only security I had.

On the other hand, I felt relief, a thawing of the tension that had been gathering for a long time. I had allowed myself to slide backward after vowing that I would change my life for good and refuse to stand on the sidelines. Now I was back on track. I would go to Mr. Bai and demand some answers. And if his solemn promise to me had meant anything, I'd get them.

TWENTY-EIGHT

I WORKED LATER THAN USUAL the next day, arriving
home mid-afternoon with an empty stomach and a case of
the jitters. Thoughts of Ninon and my status with Mr. Bai
endlessly bounced off one another. I took a longer run
than usual, pushing hard so I'd be tired and able to sleep.
Afterwards I showered and ate an early supper, then found
a not-too-stupid movie on TV, forcing myself to stay awake
until it was over. Before I turned in I checked the street for
watchers but saw nothing out of the ordinary.

I hardly ever remember my dreams, but in a nightmare
that night I found myself at the rink, flying down the ice,
the rasp of my skate blades in my ears, my stickhandling a
blur as I sidestepped bodychecks, hurtling toward the net.
All of my teammates, a row of blank faces, watched silently
from the bench. I swept to the left wing, the goalie slipping
across the crease, tracking me. Then I pivoted, zipped back

to centre, and when the goalie reacted I drilled a slapshot aimed high to the corner of the net.

But my stick broke and the puck dribbled straight to the netminder.

The dream recycled. I missed again and again, in exactly the same way. I read my failure in the faces in the crowd.

The dream cut to another scene—a penalty shot. I circled to build up speed, then came straight in on goal and flicked a wrist shot. Dead on target. Goal! A bell rang. But the red light didn't come on. The puck bounced off the mesh and ricocheted right back out to my stick. Impossible! A bell rang every time I shot and scored, but the net always spat back the puck.

"Why is there a bell?" I asked myself, circling to renew the attack. "There's no bell in hockey!"

My eyes popped open. Heart thudding, I propped myself up on one elbow. In the living room, my Curtis cell was ringing. I scrambled from the bed and ran to the phone, pushed the green button.

"Is this Julian?"

A male voice. Familiar, but I couldn't put a name to it. I shook the last images of the dream from my head. "Who is this?" I demanded.

"Are you Julian?"

"Yeah."

"I'm calling for Ninon. She needs you. Better hurry."

The taxi picked its way along dark empty streets toward the lake. It passed through shadowy pools under wide bridges and tangles of roads and ramps. It crossed desolate stretches of flat land where the bulk of an occasional building loomed above dimly lit streets. The driver drew to a halt in the middle of a block. Ahead, the road dead-ended at a stretch of hurricane fence with dark horizontal space behind it. A canal of some sort, I guessed. On one side of the road cranes reared into the moonless sky beside some sort of half-completed warehouse or factory; on the other was an open space of unlit and unused land with a few trees where a tiny light prickled in the distance.

From my shirt pocket I pulled the scrap of paper with the scribbled directions I had been given over the phone.

"This is it?" I asked.

"Yeah. We just crossed the intersection you mentioned. The south side, you said."

"Can you wait?"

The cabbie scanned the surrounding area. "Not for long."

I got out and looked around, heard a thump as the taxi's door locks engaged. Not a human form to be seen, not a vehicle on the poorly illuminated roads. A sustained hiss of light traffic on the elevated expressway behind me. Unsure of where to search, I began to walk toward the flickering light, passing through long, dry grass strewn with litter, into the spindly, ragged-looking trees. Closer, the light turned out to be a small campfire. Four silent figures sat on logs, hunched around the crackling blaze, its light glimmering on their lowered faces. Along with woodsmoke I smelled cigarettes, weed, wine.

Someone hissed, "Over here."

I followed the sound, finding a crude shelter made from a tarp stretched between trees. The shape standing beside it was one of the chess players from Grange Park. His clothing smelled of liquor and cigarettes.

"Where is she?" I asked.

He nodded to the dark space under the lean-to. "There."

Dropping to my knees, I crawled under the tarp. I made out the forms of two figures stretched out next to a bundle of clothes, giving out soft snores. I peered at them, barely able to make out their faces. One was the second chess player; the other, a woman I didn't recognize.

"She's not here," I said. "Is this some kind of—"

"That's her, right there," the guy insisted, pointing at the heap of clothes.

I crawled a few feet farther. I heard a cough. Ninon was wrapped in her camo jacket, knees to chest, head tucked down, shivering despite the warm evening. Bits of dried leaves speckled her tangled hair. Her eyes were squeezed shut, her chapped lips slightly parted, and she was breathing raggedly. The odour of dried vomit and sweat seeped from her clothes.

I turned on the chess player, but he held up his hand, cutting me off.

"Cool it, man. She wouldn't let us do nothing for her, or take her anywheres. You know what she's like. She's been here—what, a few days? Wouldn't go to the mission. Or couldn't. Then tonight she digs a phone number out of that bag of hers and asks me to call. I'm sorry, man. We done all we could. She's bad sick."

I slipped my arms under Ninon's body and got to my

feet. She was as light as a little girl. Her head lolled against my chest as I set off.

"Hold up!" said the chess player. He laid Ninon's satchel on her stomach.

The taxi was waiting just where I'd left it. When the driver saw me coming he hopped out and opened the back door. I put Ninon on the seat and ran around to the other side, got in and put my arm around her.

"Julian," she said, her whisper raspy and weak. "I knew you'd come."

And she drifted away again.

I took her home, thinking the hospital Emergency ward was probably crowded and the wait for help would be long. They might think Ninon was just another addict. At my house there was a nurse right upstairs.

I paid off the cab and carried Ninon to my apartment and laid her on the sofa, a pillow under her head. I brought her a tumbler of water but she managed only a few sips. Then I ran upstairs and tapped on Fiona's door.

"Fiona, it's Julian."

A few minutes later the door opened a crack. Fiona peered at me over the taut safety chain.

"Julian, what on earth—"

"I need your help. My friend is sick."

"What? Your—"

"Please hurry."

Fiona looked into my face, then closed the door. I heard the chain sliding in its track. The door opened.

"Put the kettle on," she said. "I'll be down in a tick."

She bustled through my door a few minutes behind me, a thin housecoat over her nightgown, a stethoscope in one hand and her first aid kit—which I had seen before, when she fixed up my face—in the other. She squeezed onto the edge of the couch.

"Shove over a wee bit, dear," she said softly. "And let's have a look at you." Then, without looking up, "Julian, tea."

"I don't think she—"

"Not for her, for me. And a couple of acetaminophen if you have them. She has a fever."

I plugged in the kettle and tossed two tea bags into the pot. While Fiona took Ninon's temperature and checked her blood pressure, I dissolved a couple of acetaminophen in half a cup of warm water. I watched anxiously as Fiona spent a long time with her stethoscope, moving it around Ninon's chest and back, repeating, "Deep breath, now." Finally, she stuffed the scope into the pocket of her robe and turned to me.

"Put lots of sugar in that, too," she told me. Then, to her patient, "What's your name, dear?"

The answer was barely audible.

"Right, come on Ninon, let's get you more upright."

We propped her up with cushions. It took a while, but she got down the water with the sugar and drug in it, then went to sleep again. Fiona tilted her head toward the kitchen. Over tea at the table she gave me the diagnosis.

"She has a high fever, not dangerous now, but potentially so. The acetaminophen will help that. What's more important, I think she has pneumonia. That's what's causing the cough, the shortness of breath and the shivers. It hurts her to breathe. Her blood pressure's a bit low—also to be expected." She lowered her voice. "She's in bad shape. We need to get her to hospital—tonight."

I jumped up. "Should I—"

"No need to panic, Julian. First, I'll give her a bath. I can lend her some clothes. I'll call Emergency and tell them she's coming. I know a couple of people on the night shift. Unless there's a big crisis, they'll get to her right away."

Relieved to be with someone who knew what she was doing, I just nodded.

"Now, let's go over a few things. You have to know what to say when you take her in. Is she a minor?"

"I don't know her exact age, but she's under eighteen for sure."

"Do you know anything about her?"

I had to tell her, even if I was giving up secrets Ninon wouldn't want told.

"She's an orphan, from Quebec. She's a street kid."

"An addict?"

"I'm almost certain she isn't."

"Okay, when they admit her, there'll be paperwork. She needs an address. Say you're her brother. Otherwise, since she's a minor, you'll have social services visiting. Maybe that would be best."

"No way."

"Alright, go with what I've said for now. The main thing is to get her in. Does she have a health card?"

"I'll check her bag. She might. I don't know."

"Now would be a good time to run the bath for her. I'll just check on Roger and be right back."

While Fiona helped Ninon into the tub behind the closed door, I picked up the clothes she had tossed into the hall. They smelled so bad I stuffed them into a plastic bag. I'd wash them later. Lifting Ninon's satchel to the kitchen table, I fought off a pang of guilt at invading her privacy, reminding myself it had to be done.

Rather than rummage around the chaos inside, I took items out one by one and laid them on the table—her diary, two pairs of clean socks, a couple of novels, a few pairs of clean panties rolled up and held tight by a scrunchie, a big plastic comb, a small bundle of photos in an envelope, a packet of tampons, miscellaneous gum and candy wrappers and then the prize. A small zippered bag. Inside were a Certificate of Canadian Residency, a Quebec Health Insurance card, her French passport. I had all I needed to get her into the hospital with no strings. I put the certificate and health card into my backpack with my two cells and went to knock on the bathroom door.

"Fiona, should I call an ambulance?"

Her reply was tight. "No need. A taxi."

I did as she said, adding a book to my pack. I figured it would be a long night.

TWENTY-NINE

Fiona had made it happen.

An hour and a half later I was sitting in a chair beside Ninon, who lay sleeping fitfully on a gurney parked tightly against the wall of a narrow hallway in the crowded Emergency ward. A tube snaked up to a bag of clear liquid hanging on a rack rising from the corner of the gurney. How she was able to sleep in the din, I didn't know. The corridor was a carnival of voices, bustling men and women in green scrubs or white coats, groans and cries of discomfort and pain from other gurneys lining the walls.

I was now Ninon's next of kin, her half-brother. The admitting secretary, a sour-faced, impatient woman, had almost caught me out of position when I told her Ninon was my sister. She commented, "Hmm, brother and sister with different surnames."

But I came back fast. "Different fathers," I said. Next

came my address and phony names for our non-existent parents, who were away on holiday, touring South America.

"They're out of touch for a few days," I said, adding to the pile of lies.

In the hallway, I sat with one arm resting on the cot, my hand in Ninon's, holding my novel and trying without much success to read. Time seemed to disappear. I wasn't wearing a watch and there was no clock in the corridor. Ninon floated in and out of awareness. She already looked a bit better. She wasn't so pale and her lips had a blush of colour now. But every breath was an effort as she dragged the air in and pushed it out again. I got up and for the hundredth time kissed her forehead.

After a long while a passing nurse stopped by the gurney and consulted a clipboard, then checked the name tag on the frame of the cot.

"Ninon Bisset," he said.

I nodded.

"We're going to take her for some tests. You might as well have a break, see if you can find a place to sit in the waiting room. Check with the desk in about an hour and a half. After the tests, we'll be putting her in a room. You can see her there when we have her set up. Any questions?"

"She'll be okay, right?"

"The doctor will talk to you after the results come in."

He rolled Ninon down the hall and they disappeared into an elevator.

I made my way to the waiting room. It was jammed, hot and depressing, so I went outside and sat down on a low wall outside the door and watched the traffic lights change on the street corner across the way. I couldn't forget

Fiona's tight-lipped expression when she brought Ninon out of the steamy bathroom. She had noticed something about Ninon, something that wasn't good. And she hadn't told me what it was.

Just after dawn a volunteer senior at Information directed me to the seventh floor. I found Ninon's room easily enough. It was past the nursing station, at the end of the hall. Her bed, by the window, was the only one in a room that smelled of chemicals and wax.

She lay asleep, cradled by pillows, her eyes closed, her thick hair combed back, her skin wan and papery. She seemed captured and trapped by the chrome bed rails, at the mercy of strangers and machines and the illness that held her down and stole her breath. An IV pierced the back of each hand, delivering blood to one and glucose to the other. Connected to an oxygen receptacle in the wall behind her, a hose fed into a plastic tubular head harness with a tiny vent under each nostril.

The sight of her filled me with dread. That can't be Ninon, I thought. Ninon has always been as free as a breeze, now here, now there, with me one minute and away the next, with the sun glowing on her skin and a sparkle in her eyes.

I stood at the foot of her bed, replaying in my mind the image of Fiona's face last night, just before I phoned for the taxi. I struggled to bring myself under control, then called Ninon's name. Her eyelids fluttered, then opened, the green irises bright with fever.

"*Julien*," she rasped, using the French pronunciation.

"I'm here."

"I'm in the hospital?"

"I brought you in last night."

"Is there water?"

I filled a tumbler from the water pitcher on her bedside table and stuck a bendable straw into it and held it to her mouth. After she got down some water her voice was stronger.

"How am I?"

"You have pneumonia and a fever. That's all I know so far. But you're safe now; you'll be taken care of."

"All my joints ache *et j'ai un mal de tête*."

"I can fetch the nurse."

"Don't go," she said, closing her eyes. A moment later she was breathing evenly.

I left the room and walked down the hall to the nursing station. A man and woman, both in baggy blue outfits, were doing paperwork at a small counter under a row of cupboards. When she noticed me the woman came to the window.

"I'm Ninon Bisset's brother," I told her. "Could you tell me how she is? I mean, what's wrong with her?"

The nurse smiled and said, "She has double pneumonia. We're treating her for that and for fever. And we're waiting for test results."

Her musical Caribbean accent was calming.

"What are you testing her for?"

"Just routine."

Which was what the cops in the novels always said when a person being questioned asked, "What's all this about?" The reply meant the cops didn't want to reveal information. Or couldn't because they didn't know the answers themselves.

"Any chance you'll tell me what 'routine' means?"

She smiled again. "As soon as more information comes in a doctor will speak with you."

I thanked her, then continued down the hall to a small lounge I had noticed on the way in. It was empty. I called the store. Mrs. Altan didn't seem convinced by my sick relative excuse. After checking the Chang cell for a message and finding none, I returned to Ninon's room and sat down in the chair between the window and bed. I felt useless. The room was hot, the air stale and dry. I yawned, reached for my book, tried to concentrate on the words on the page. I read the same paragraph four times before giving up.

A janitor with a mop and a bucket on wheels came by and asked me to give him a few minutes to swab the floors—which looked clean to me. But I nodded and went to the lounge again. I flipped through a couple of two-year-old yachting magazines. When I returned, stepping past the bright yellow "Caution: Slippery Floor" sign in front of the door, the guy with the pail had gone. Someone had hung new IV bags on the poles and fluffed up Ninon's pillows.

Suddenly I felt an overwhelming surge of gratitude to the people caring for her, the men and women on her case. They knew what they were doing, I told myself. They'd help her. She'd be okay.

I kissed Ninon on the forehead, drew my chair closer to her bed, lowered the side frame, laid my head on my forearms, and within minutes I slid into a troubled sleep.

———

Ninon woke a few times during the morning. We talked a bit, but she found it hard to concentrate. Every little while she whispered, "Stay with me," and I would try to reassure her. Lunchtime came. She drank some juice and managed a few spoons of jelly. Lunchtime went. A couple of orderlies came in, uncoupled her oxygen tube, released the brakes on her bed and wheeled her away down the hall to the elevator. Taking her for more tests, they told me. While she was gone the Chang cell vibrated in my pocket. I took the call in the lounge.

A text message from "Number Withheld" read "Pickup 9:00 am tomorrow."

"I guess I've got my meeting with Mr. Bai," I told the empty room.

I didn't care anymore.

It was dark when I plodded up the stairs to my apartment and let myself in. I poured the coffee I had bought on the way home into a cup and put it into the microwave, then carried the bag containing Ninon's clothes down to the basement and dumped them into the washer/dryer.

The smell of the hot coffee when I returned to the kitchen reminded me that I had eaten next to nothing all day beyond half a cheese sandwich that tasted like plastic-wrapped cardboard. I found a can of beef stew in the cupboard and heated it on the stove and ate it with some soda crackers. Before I turned in I called the hospital and asked for the nursing station on the seventh floor.

"This is Ninon Bisset's brother," I said. "How is she doing?"

The male nurse on the other end said, "Since you left her less than an hour ago? She's resting comfortably."

Resting comfortably. Did these people get their dialogue from TV shows? Then I told myself I wasn't being fair.

"Do you have my phone number handy?"

He read the number to me.

"That's it. I'm being a pain, aren't I?"

The nurse chuckled. "You're okay. Pain is why we're here."

I crawled into bed and listened to the crickets in the yard. Damn, I thought. I didn't check the street before I came to bed.

"Ah, if they're watching, let them," I said to the crickets.

THIRTY

As soon as I woke up I called the hospital—a busy time on the ward. Doctors' rounds, breakfast, pill distribution and more.

I was folding Ninon's clothes and putting them in her canvas bag when Fiona knocked on my door on her way to drop Roger at Trish's place.

"Any news?" she asked, shushing Roger, who was squirming in her arms.

"I'm not getting any information out of anyone," I replied. "That's bad, isn't it? I mean, if there was good news, they'd tell me, right?"

Roger was babbling and crushing Fiona's uniform collar in his little fists as she spoke.

"Not bad, no. Professional. The doctors don't want to tell you anything concrete until they've collected all the data they can. It's not fair to the patient to make surmises that might be misleading or even wrong. I know it's hard, Julian. You'll probably hear something solid today."

"I hope so," I said.

Making her way down the stairs, one hand on the bannister and the other around Roger's waist, Fiona turned back.

"Ninon's lucky to have a friend like you," she said.

I was washing the breakfast dishes when a car pulled into the driveway, right on time. On my way out I grabbed Ninon's satchel. She'd need her own clothes when the hospital discharged her. Chang wasn't in the car. I said hello to the driver, who wasn't sporting his uniform and peaked cap this time. He nodded, then reversed into the street and drove off.

I pushed my thoughts away from Ninon and toward the upcoming meeting with Mr. Bai—the discussion I had insisted on. Now it didn't seem so important. I rehearsed what I wanted to say and learn, plagued by doubts and second guesses. Would Mr. Bai make things clear for me or would he get angry and back out of our deal? Did I really want to know the answers to my questions?

A lot had happened since last March, when Chang had picked me up on the street near my school and taken me to the quiet, expensively furnished office above the Happy Garden restaurant. I lived in my own apartment, I had become a sort of building superintendent and handyman, I worked part-time at the convenience store, all thanks to Mr. Bai. Although Curtis's assignments were separate, they were a direct result of Bai's finding me the job at the QuickMart.

But I had also landed in the middle of a mysterious operation that had escalated into a dark scenario involving watchers, covert entry and bugging, and Charr's scary escape in the middle of the night. I didn't even know what or who Charr had been trying to avoid.

Well, I thought, as the car pulled into the parking lot and came to a smooth stop at the restaurant's side door, maybe after this morning it will be all over.

In one way or another.

The three of us, Mr. Bai, Chang and I, sat in the same leather chairs in front of the fireplace, the little red clay pot of tea on the coffee table between Bai and me. On my right, Chang sat calmly, ready to provide simultaneous translation.

I searched Bai's face for any sign of what was to come. Was he angry with me, impatient with my demand? I couldn't tell. His smooth oval face held no expression. Even so, the aura of power and authority was there, a contrast to his small stature, his bright almond-shaped eyes, his manicured nails and costly clothing.

Once the polite niceties were out of the way—all of Bai's words coming in Chinese and turned into elegant English by Chang—Bai blindsided me.

"I am sorry to hear that your friend is unwell," he said. "You must not hesitate if there is anything I can do."

A few seconds passed before I realized he had spoken in perfect, unaccented English.

"Thank you," I replied mechanically, my thoughts racing to catch up with this latest twist. What had been the point of the laborious time-wasting charade of our first meeting, when every word that travelled across the coffee table had to be said twice? Was it a power move on Mr. Bai's part? A way of dominating the conversation? Was it tradition or custom?

Chang piped up. "Julian, you have expressed a desire to ask Mr. Bai some questions about the guests occasionally permitted to stay at his house. He understands that you harbour certain doubts in connection with these guests and he has agreed to answer your questions."

I wondered why Chang had to be so formal, so stuffy when he talked. Trying to impress his boss? I replied by nodding.

"Before he does, I remind you that Mr. Bai and his arrangements are to be kept in strict confidence, or as we say, *shou kou ru ping*—make your mouth a sealed bottle."

I nodded again, fed up with Chang's wordiness.

"He has asked me to add that he especially appreciates your help with Li Ai-wen, the gentleman whom you assisted not long ago. Now, you may go ahead."

Throughout Chang's blathering I had kept my eyes on Bai sitting comfortably in his chair. When Chang fell silent I said nothing for a few moments, casting about for a place to begin. So far I had felt like a little boy coming to his grandpa to ask for a couple of bucks to buy ice cream. The two men in the room with me, polite and formal and businesslike, had purposely created an atmosphere where I was a distant third in importance. I didn't care about status, but I didn't like being shoved around.

I said, "One of the people who stayed at the house works at Mama Zhu's restaurant. Are you a human smuggler?"

My bombshell stunned both of them. A shroud of silence fell over the room. Bai stared at me. Chang's mouth dropped but he recovered quickly.

"Yes," Bai said.

My turn to be caught off guard. In one go I had fired off all the bullets in my clip, and I had nothing more to say. I fell back on an old strategy. When in doubt, keep your mouth shut. It was Bai's turn.

He smiled. Gotcha right back, his smile seemed to say.

"I am indeed a smuggler. But not in the way you might think. Your observation of the young woman being trained in the Chongqing Gardens kitchen persuaded you that she is an illegal immigrant. She is, as are all the others. Mr. Li, whom you kindly assisted recently, is also an illegal."

I killed a few seconds by lifting my cup and taking in a few sips of green tea. Bai did the same.

"You may have thought I am what we call a snakehead—the boss of a criminal gang. I understand how you came to that conclusion, and I acknowledge that the secrecy I have imposed on Mr. Chang and others has contributed to your confusion and put you at some risk. But I assure you, you were never in danger.

"Let me put it this way, Julian. The guests are illegal until we can get them registered as refugees, which is becoming increasingly difficult. In the meantime I provide them with jobs and a place to stay. All of them except Mr. Li—I'll get to his case in a moment—come from the area around my home village in north China. They were obliged to flee the country because they got into trouble with corrupt local officials who have the power to jail them for an indefinite period, or possibly worse. A few villagers have even been murdered. It all has to do with criminal business practices involving everything from dangerous coal mines to unregulated factories.

"You must understand that my homeland is not a society of law. I support an organization in the area—what you might call a secret human rights group. The people who used the house where you live as a temporary resting place have all had harrowing journeys just to get to this country."

Mr. Bai went on to relate Charr's—Li Ai-wen's—tale. He was a writer, a novelist, who had been imprisoned along with his wife ten years ago for criticizing the Chinese government, especially the Communist Party. His books were banned in China but published in other countries in translation. Li's wife was a journalist who got into trouble for advocating democracy.

A year before I met Mr. Bai, Li was awarded the Green Ribbon Prize, a European literary award almost as famous as the Nobel Prize. The Chinese government, fearing worldwide criticism and a massive loss of face for holding the prize-winner in jail, released him. That was when he learned his wife had died in prison—four years before.

The government wouldn't let him travel to Europe to collect the prize. They pretended he was free but he was really under house arrest. Li knew that he'd be imprisoned again as soon as the prize was no longer in the news. When he was secretly approached by Mr. Bai's contacts, he agreed to try to get out.

"You mean the authorities let him believe his wife was still alive for four years?" I asked.

Both men nodded.

"So you see, Julian," Bai summed up, "what I am doing by helping these people get into this country is illegal, but it is not immoral."

I believed him. And with that, my attitude toward him took a new turn. He wasn't a criminal. He wasn't exploiting refugees for cheap labour; he was helping desperate people escape to a better life, just as he had assisted me. And I felt a connection, now, to the faceless men and women who appeared and disappeared at my house. They needed a river. I didn't see them as a possible threat to my safety anymore. They had done what I had done, but for them it was dangerous. They were brave. They had ripped themselves free from their roots and homes and launched themselves toward a future they could hardly imagine. In doing that they had trusted the man across the table from me—and he had come through for them.

Mr. Bai drank more tea and settled back, waiting for the next question.

"Who are the watchers, then? And who broke into the house and planted the bugs?" I asked. "It seems like some of them were amateurs and some were pros."

"Unfortunately our Mr. Li, being a man of international reputation, attracted a great deal of attention here as well as elsewhere when he disappeared from his house in China. None of the watchers as you call them were immigration officials or police. All were connected in one way or another with the Chinese embassy here in this country."

"The embassy? But—"

"And once again you have been very observant. The watchers fall into two groups, as you point out. The professionals, those behind the surreptitious entry and listening devices, are directly in the employ of the Chinese embassy in Ottawa, through the consulate here in this city. All embassies have what you might call an espionage department. They spy on the host country from within. China maintains an extensive and very effective information-gathering program here. Mr. Li is a renowned figure and his escape is a source of great embarrassment for China. China wants him back, in jail. If they could get him to the embassy they might be able to do that.

"Most men and women we bring into this country are much smaller fish. China simply wants to keep track of them, and does so through the clubs and organizations in the Chinese expatriate communities. Cultural groups and the like. The watchers are volunteers who co-operate with the consulate here in the city. They are, as you say, amateurs."

"Okay, I understand," I said. "All that makes sense. It seems selfish of me, now that I see how you're helping these people, but if I'm in the middle of all this illegal activity— even if it isn't immoral—I could lose everything. I'm a runaway too."

"Lately we have been closely pressed and had little choice but to use the house to help Li Ai-wen. But we have altered our methodology as of Mr. Li's escape. You will see no more illegal guests at the house. Or at least not for a long time."

I sipped more tea, suddenly anxious to get out of there and rush over to the hospital.

"Thanks for clearing all that up," I said.

Bai stood up. "Not at all, Julian. I am grateful for the help with Mr. Li. You did a good thing." He smiled. "It seems fate has sent you to my assistance again."

"Please say goodbye to him for me," I said.

"You may rely on me to do so."

Chang escorted me out to the car. "Can the driver drop me at the hospital?" I asked.

Chang fired off directions to the driver and the car slid into the traffic on Dundas, heading east. I was relieved but tried not to think about what had just happened, what I had learned from Mr. Bai. It was all too much to take in. Since I had picked up Ninon two nights ago and brought her home and learned how sick she was, her health had occupied all my mental energy. Fiona had said that today I might finally learn exactly what was wrong with Ninon. I hoped so.

And, in a way, I hoped not.

THIRTY-ONE

IT WAS LATE MORNING when I slipped into Ninon's room. I found her propped higher in bed, the IVs in place, the oxygen harness looped behind her ears, passing under her nose. She was awake, and the sight of her lifted my spirits and calmed my nerves. She looked good. Her face wasn't so pale, her eyes were once more Ninon's beautiful green, without the false glimmer of fever.

I was so relieved I felt weak in the knees.

"I should have brought you a box of chocolates," I said. "Or some roses."

"I don't like roses, and chocolates give me zits. A kiss will do."

Her voice was still a little bit raspy and low, like a breeze moving through dried grass. Between sentences she paused briefly. We talked for a while about not very much. Then we got around to the night I brought her home.

"Now you know where I slept when the mission was full or I had maxed out my stay," she said.

"It seems a little dangerous."

"I know. But it isn't as bad as it looks. All the other people there are regulars like me. We keep the place a secret. It's off the beaten path. We sort of look out for one another."

"Why did you wait for so long to get in touch?"

"I got so weak I kind of lost direction. I guess I wasn't thinking too clearly."

Ninon was tiring, her strength already used up, so I lowered the side of the bed and sat holding her hand. In a few moments her eyelids slipped down and her shallow breathing grew more regular.

I was encouraged by her improvement. She was still weak, but her colouring and strength—even if it didn't last long—showed she was on the mend. I guessed the antibiotics were doing what they were supposed to do.

After a while I took the elevator back to the first floor and bought a coffee and doughnut at the cafeteria. I sat at one of the tables and read a newspaper someone had left behind, but I couldn't absorb anything. My Curtis phone rang.

"Gulun is mad at you," Curtis reported.

I had forgotten to call the store and tell the Altans I wouldn't be in.

"I'll call him right now," I said. "Thanks for the heads-up."

"I could use your help. I've signed up a new client whose fifteen-year-old son is—"

"Sorry, Curtis. I gotta take care of something. I won't be available for a few days at least."

"You sound a little . . . listen, Julian, I'll pass the message on to Gulun for you."

"Thanks," I said, and ended the call.

I finished the cold coffee and semi-stale doughnut. When I got off the elevator at Ninon's floor a woman in white holding a clipboard was coming out of the nursing station. She saw me and waited.

"Mr. Paladin?"

She was a head shorter than me, with large brown eyes and a cool professional manner.

"I'm Doctor Mody," she said. "Let's go into the lounge where we can talk."

My stomach dropped. I followed her down the hall, my heart leaping in my chest. The lounge was unoccupied. Dr. Mody shut the door and showed me to a seat, then she perched on the arm of the couch opposite. The wall behind her was barred with yellow light coming through the window blinds.

She consulted the clipboard. "You're Ms. Bisset's brother, or rather, half-brother."

"Yes."

"And I gather your parents are in South America and out of touch for a few days."

"That's right. Last time I spoke with them they were in, er, Chile."

She made a note. "Well, you're eighteen. I suppose that makes you her de facto legal guardian and proximate next of kin."

I nodded and linked my fingers in my lap to keep them from trembling.

In a softer voice, she continued. "You know your sister is very sick."

"Pneumonia," I replied weakly.

"It's much more than pneumonia, I'm afraid. Mr. Paladin,

has your sister shown signs of fatigue for the last while?"

My mind raced over memories of the times I had been with Ninon.

"Yes, she has."

"Weakness?"

"Yes."

"Weight loss?"

"I guess so."

Where was she leading me? What was she working up to? Whatever it was, I didn't want to hear it. I wanted out of that tiny, closed-in space.

"Has she ever manifested night sweats, headaches, irritability?"

I gulped. "We don't see each other that often."

Dr. Mody made another note, which made me feel guilty. Had I missed something with Ninon, something that would have told me—what? I realized the doctor wasn't really pumping me for information. She was taking me through Ninon's symptoms, preparing me for what was to come.

"Mr. Paladin, tests confirm that your sister has acute myeloid leukemia. That's cancer of the bone marrow, and it means her blood has an extremely elevated level of white blood cells. White blood cells in a healthy body repel and defeat disease. In Ninon's case, she has so many that her body in a sense attacks itself. One of the side effects is that the body loses much of its ability to fight infection. Hence the pneumonia. Do you understand?"

"Yes," I whispered, my eyes on my hands.

"Miss Bisset's—Ninon's—illness is well advanced. Her spleen is enlarged. Her bone marrow is severely compromised."

Shut up! Stop! I screamed inside my skull. My chest

heaved as I clawed for breath. I forced myself to speak.

"What do you need to do?"

"In some cases we would seek out a donor and perform a bone marrow transplant—"

"I'll do it! I'll be a donor!"

"Mr. Paladin, sometimes, by the time we're called in, the disease has progressed so far it cannot be arrested. I'm afraid that in Ninon's case there is nothing we can do."

Her words hung in the air like bitter smoke. They didn't register. I waited for her to continue, to outline a plan to bring Ninon back. But she didn't. She sat there, quiet and serious, clutching her clipboard. She waited. And finally her words formed in my mind, seeping into my understanding like another lethal disease.

"Doctor," I begged. "Please. No."

"We'll do all we can to make her comfortable."

Don't make her comfortable! Make her well!

I felt tears on my cheeks. "There must be something," I pleaded. "Please. You can't just leave her to . . ." I trailed off, then whispered, "I can't lose her. I can't."

"I'm very sorry, Mr. Paladin."

The room was silent, airless. I could hardly breathe.

"Does she know?"

"I spoke to her just before you came by the nursing station."

I nodded.

Dr. Mody rose and went to the door. "I'll leave you alone for a few minutes. Perhaps you'd like to call your family."

She left, letting the door close behind her.

I fell back into the chair. Family? Who could I call? Who would answer?

———

I stood outside Ninon's room, too terrified to step across the threshold. My heart thrummed hollowly in my ears, my lungs tugged in small gulps of air. What should I say to her? Where should I begin? I couldn't stand beside her bed with a stuffed teddy bear in one hand and a bouquet of daisies in the other and mumble worn-out phrases like How are they treating you today? or When will you be coming home? All that was gone now. The doctor had swept aside Ninon's future the way you'd brush a crumb off the table with a flick of your hand.

The rustle of cloth behind me, and the squeaky wheels of a medication trolley, rallied my thoughts. I couldn't help Ninon get better. All I could do was be with her. I went into the room.

Her eyes were open, unfocused, turned slightly toward the window. I wanted to pull away the needles and tubes, take her into my arms and carry her out of there to some-where safe. Instead I kissed her on the forehead, then on her dry lips. She reached up, hooked her arms around me fiercely and held me so tightly she lifted herself off the mattress for a second.

The effort exhausted her. She let her arms fall across her chest, the backs of her hands purple with bruises from the IVs. I made myself look into her eyes, where tears gathered and overflowed, running across her temples and into her hair. Her voice was barely audible.

"They told you?"

I nodded, unable to speak, and kissed her again and buried my face in the pillow beside hers, felt her arms around me again, her hair against my cheek.

"Don't cry," she whispered. "Don't."

THIRTY-TWO

I SLIPPED THROUGH the following days like a shadow, unconnected to the world except when I was in Ninon's room. In the mornings I walked along the streets to the hospital, barely conscious of my surroundings. When visiting hours were over in the evenings, I reversed the journey. I couldn't have described the weather or the traffic on Coxwell Avenue or the brief conversations I had with Rawlins and Fiona as I came and went.

I spent every minute I could with Ninon. As time passed I watched her fade, each day losing ground to her disease, powerless to defend herself. Seeing her driven helplessly toward her fate, unable to help her, was a prison sentence in hell. If ever I had wondered what it was like to love someone, I didn't anymore.

Ninon was swept by gusts of emotion. One day she'd seem confident she could get better, the next, resigned to her short future. And sometimes bitterness overwhelmed her.

"I finally found someone," she said one rainy afternoon, "but it's too late."

As I made my way back home that evening, her words echoed inside my head like the ticks and tocks of an old mantel clock. It was a dirty trick, she had gone on to say. God must be laughing at us.

But most of the time she didn't have the energy to be angry. And then one day as I hugged her before leaving she whispered, "Julian, I don't want to die here. Take me home."

That night I knocked on Fiona's door. She let me in and sat me down and poured me a cup of tea. Fiona was a pro. She saw death all the time. She didn't try to sugar-coat things, but she was comforting.

I talked for a long time. I told her I wanted to bring Ninon home to my apartment, that it was Ninon's wish. Could I manage it?

Fiona stirred her tea. "The hospital might not want to discharge her. Ninon is a minor."

"Even if it's what she wants?"

"Their job is to care for her. If they think she won't get proper care from you, they'll object. Plus, they won't want to be legally liable if they discharge Ninon without assurance that she'll get competent help."

We sidestepped that problem for a while and discussed what I'd need in the way of supplies—bandages, IVs and so on. Then I brought us back on track.

"How can I persuade them? What do I need to do?"

Fiona thought for a moment.

"It would help if you said you had hired a home-care nurse to assist in looking after her."

"Okay, I'll look into that. Where should I go?"

She smiled. "You needn't go far."

"But what about your job at the hospital?"

"I'll be able to look in on her when I'm home."

I had a thought. "If the hospital gives me trouble, would a lawyer help?"

"It wouldn't hurt," she replied. "Now listen, Julian. Before you make a final decision, you need to know that when Ninon gets near the end it won't be pretty. You know she already has help using a bedpan. She'll need to be washed, and you'll have to be on the watch for bedsores. The worst is that you'll see every step in her deterioration. It's not like the movies. It can be ugly and smelly and . . . well, nobody would blame you if you decided to let Ninon stay in palliative care."

"It's what she wants," I said.

"The hospital staff is equipped, materially and emotionally."

"But they don't love her."

That night I called the lawyer whose name was on the card Chang had given me the day he presented me with my new identity. The lawyer asked lots of questions. We talked for more than half an hour. He said he'd take care of everything, that he foresaw no problems. He even agreed to arrange for a standby home-care nurse for times when Fiona wasn't around.

In the morning I told Ninon that I had to take a couple of hours to lay in the medical and other supplies. I'd be bringing her home the next day. The news brought a smile to her lips.

"Just you and me," she whispered.

"Keep it to yourself for now," I said.

I returned to the hospital just as the orderlies were wheeling the big food-tray racks away toward the elevator. Luckily, Dr. Mody was at the nursing station talking to the Jamaican nurse, who I thought, for some reason, might be on my side when they heard what I had to say. I got right to the point, thanking the doctor for her help and informing her that I'd be taking Ninon home.

She objected, listing all the reasons why this course of action wasn't possible, growing more heated each time I stated my intention and repeated that Ninon didn't want to face the end in a hospital. I didn't argue, I just kept at it. The more the doctor protested, the more I admired her. She wanted what she thought was best for Ninon.

Finally, she fell back on authority. "I'm not going to discharge her and that's that."

Through it all the nurse looked on silently, her face empty of expression.

I went into Ninon's room. She had rallied a bit since the morning. Fiona had warned me there would be times when I'd think Ninon was getting better, that she would feel stronger, but these encouraging moments were temporary.

"I hate to say so, Julian," Fiona reminded me, "but this can only go one way."

The lawyer, George Wang, a tall man in a dark suit, arrived around six-thirty toting a fat soft-sided briefcase. With him was another man, as short as the lawyer was tall, as thickset as the lawyer was trim. Wang introduced him as Mr. Bo, his assistant. We shook hands in the hallway, then Wang went to work.

He walked over to the nursing station, asked for the person in charge, presented his card and said he was about to confer with his clients, Ms. Bisset and Mr. Paladin, and must not, barring an emergency, be disturbed. The doctor on shift nodded and turned back to his charts.

In Ninon's room, with the door closed, Wang spoke to Ninon, who was awake and alert. I stood beside the bed, holding her hand. As the question-and-answer session went on, Wang assured himself that Ninon was in control of her words and thoughts and understood everything he said.

Sets of papers with coloured triangles stapled to the upper left corners were produced, explained, and signed by all four of us—the two "principals," then Mr. Wang as counsel and Mr. Bo as witness. Wang placed one set in his briefcase, left two on Ninon's table and, after saying goodbye to Ninon and assuring her he'd see her again at my apartment in a couple of days, took the fourth set to the nursing station.

This time a different doctor greeted him. He was grey-haired, with a kindly face. Wang presented him with the papers.

"These documents indicate that, as Ms. Bisset's legal guardian"—I noticed he didn't say "half-brother"—"Mr. Paladin has taken a decision to remove her from your care with his deep gratitude, and he hereby serves notice of his decision. Ms. Bisset concurs and has so indicated in her statement. Please have the appropriate releases ready for Mr. Paladin's signature as soon as possible."

The doctor took the forms and nodded.

"We all agree, I think," added Wang, "that time is of the essence."

He snapped shut the clasp of his briefcase.

"If there are no questions . . ."

Four hours later, I carried Ninon upstairs and into my apartment.

THIRTY-THREE

I HAD MOVED MY BED to the living room, setting it opposite my reading chair so Ninon would be able to see out the bay windows to the street. I had guessed that she wouldn't want to be alone in my little bedroom. I would sleep on the couch so I'd be close by if she needed me during the night.

Soon after I got her set up, Fiona dropped by and showed me how to change the bag on the glucose feed—the blood IV was no longer necessary—and change out the oxygen cylinder when necessary.

"You could get a job as an orderly," Fiona said, smiling.

"No, he couldn't," Ninon said in her whispery voice. "He keeps kissing the patient."

I learned how to take Ninon's temperature and blood pressure, how to preheat the bedpan with hot water before taking it to the bedside, how to make jelly as well as vegetable and meat broths. I kept track of the time and administered her medication on schedule.

I read to Ninon from *Captain Alatriste*, the first in my favourite series.

"I hope the story isn't too long," Ninon joked. "I don't want to miss the end."

One early evening, Rawlins knocked on my door, his new black guitar in one hand and a beer in the other.

"Wanted to meet your guest," he said with an embarrassed smile. "Thought a little bluegrass might cheer her up."

He grabbed a kitchen chair and set it in front of the window so he'd be in Ninon's line of sight. He introduced himself and went into a jokey patter about how I had sent all the way to Nashville for him so he could give a private concert to the prettiest girl in the country. He sang a couple of songs—all upbeat, happy tunes. No whining Appalachian laments, no my-baby's-gone-and-left-me blues.

Ninon brightened immediately, smiling and humming along when she could. I slipped upstairs and invited Fiona and Roger to join us.

"Right you are," Fiona said. "The bairn's asleep so I'll leave our door open in case he stirs."

We had a sort of party, what Ninon called a *fête de la musique*. At one point Rawlins stopped playing and took a swig of his beer.

"Time for the guest of honour to sing one," he announced, his eyes on Ninon.

"I can't," she rasped.

"I can hear you just fine," Rawlins insisted. "Anything you like. Just start in and I'll pick up on it."

To my surprise, Ninon gave it a shot. We could barely hear the words scraping from her throat. She was singing in French, and the tune sounded vaguely familiar. Rawlins played along softly, picking each note so as not to drown out her frail voice. He hummed. Then Fiona joined in.

And I recognized the song. It was "Frère Jacques," a simple tune about a sleeping brother and church bells in the morning. Like a million little kids, I had picked it up at school. Ninon must have learned it too, back in her hometown in France. Recalling the words, I began to sing with her and Fiona and Rawlins.

Frère Jacques, frère Jacques,
Dormez-vous? Dormez-vous?
Sonnez les matines! . . .

I watched Ninon following Rawlins's fingers on the strings. Then she looked my way, her green eyes bright as she sang.

It was enough to break your heart.

A couple of nights after the fête Ninon asked me to come and sit by her. "Bring my diary," she whispered.

I did as she asked, sat by her bed, my knees against the mattress. She told me to turn to a blank page in the diary. She wanted me to write down her wishes for what to do "after," and went on to dictate a short list of instructions.

"I know it will be hard. Will you do it for me?"

Unable to speak, I nodded.

Fiona had warned me how I'd know it was time.

"Her blood pressure will drop," she had said, "and she'll go into a deep sleep, almost like a coma. She won't respond to your voice, but lots of people believe that the patient can feel your touch."

"Okay," I replied.

Since the day she had told me what she wanted me to do "after," Ninon seemed to relax. She said she was ready. Her choices were all gone; there were no new challenges or dangers around the corner, no unanswered questions. We fell into a daily routine.

Ninon encouraged me to take my regular run, but I didn't want to leave her for long. I'd walk up to the Danforth to do some shopping, or slip outside when she was sleeping and busy myself with pulling weeds and cultivating the flower beds. Eventually, I didn't leave the apartment at all.

Most of the time Ninon dozed, and her periods of sleep grew longer and deeper. Her body seemed to waste away, to retreat into itself—her cheeks and eyes sunken, her arms thinner, her hair dry and without the lustre it once had. But her spirit, that sense of freedom and independence that had always defined her, was still there. Still there, but tired.

When she was awake we chatted a little, often returning to the same theme. We were orphans. We had struggled to leave the past behind us, and we had pulled it off. We had found each other, if only for a short while.

We relived the few times we had had together—the art gallery, the French movie, lunch at the Chongqing Gardens, and especially the first trip to the harbour islands when we had slept the night through on the beach, with heat lightning trembling behind the clouds.

"I think we would have stayed together," Ninon said.

"Me too."

The next afternoon Ninon woke from a two-hour nap. I gave her some apple juice and as I held the glass to her lips she covered my hand with hers.

"*Julien*," she whispered, her eyes on mine.

My heart shifted. No, I thought, not yet.

"Alright," I said.

I refused to let myself think. I concentrated on the moment, the task at hand. I set the glass down and stood to shut off the glucose feed, then carefully slipped the needle from the back of Ninon's hand.

"I'm going to leave the oxygen on, okay?"

Her voice was a breath. "Yes."

I brought the blood pressure monitor to the bed and took a reading. Her pressure was falling.

"Do you want to listen to some music?" I asked.

She nodded, then said, "Make me look better."

I brought the clock radio from the bedroom and set it on my reading table and tuned it to a classical music station. I helped Ninon into a fresh nightie, rinsed her face with a damp cloth and brushed her hair.

"Ready for the dance," I said, making her smile.

I sat with her, checking her pressure every half-hour or so. It continued to fall.

"No more," she said.

I put the machine away. At ten o'clock I turned out all the lights except the reading lamp. I turned my back on Ninon for a second to shut off the radio. I heard her say, "*Julien, je t'aime.*"

In a panic, I whipped around and bent over her. She was breathing deeply and evenly. I sat on the edge of the bed, gently rubbing her forearm. And then, without opening her eyes, she breathed, "I'm cold," and rolled onto her side. I took off my jeans and T-shirt and got under the covers. I spooned up to Ninon to warm her, my arm around her waist, her head under my chin. I felt the faint rise and fall of her breathing. As the minutes passed the breaths she took grew shallower and further apart, as if she was gathering herself.

"*Maman. Papa. Julien,*" she whispered and drew in some air, hesitated, then let it go with a long sigh that told me she was gone.

L'ISLE-SUR-LA-SORGUE

There must be a highway,
There must be a train,
There must be a river
To take me away.

—Thad Rawlins

THIRTY-FOUR

My plane bumped down in Marseille about ten-thirty in the morning. Under a blinding sun I found the car that had been left for me in the parking lot, courtesy of Bai's contact, and fished the keys from under the seat. Up until now I had never driven a car without an instructor sitting beside me. Rattled by the strangeness of the place—the traffic, signs, even the design of the roads—I headed northwest, away from the coast of the Mediterranean and into the hills of Provence. I cruised through villages and small towns with shaded squares and narrow streets. With a range of mountains in the distance, the road followed the Durance River, then angled north. About mid-afternoon, eyes sandy with fatigue, I motored across a bridge into the town whose name I knew by heart. I found my hotel beside the river, where a dam formed a basin and the river split into streams, climbed the stairs to my room, locked the door and shed my clothes. Thirteen hours or so after I'd left home I slipped into bed and fell into a deep sleep.

Early next morning, well rested, I was on the road again, heading upriver through countryside showing more shades of green than I could have imagined. I came to a small village, parked in the leafy central square by the river, and trudged along a pathway that led into steeply rising hills where a crumbling ruin clung to the top of a rocky crag. The valley narrowed to a wooded gorge, the hills sharpened into cliffs, the river broke up into a long shaded fall of tumbling streams—a confusion of boulders and fallen tree trunks, rocky shelves and steps coated with moss. The cool air was heavy with the odour of vegetation and water. Finally I came to the source of the Sorgue River, called Fontaine-de-Vaucluse, a bottomless translucent green pool enclosed on three sides by sheer walls of rock soaring skyward. My guidebook claimed it was one of the most abundant sources of water in the world.

I sat on a huge boulder, cocooned by the peaceful solitude. I had never been to a place where a river was being born right before my eyes.

After a while I made my way back to the car. A kid was fly fishing from the narrow bridge near the square, his rod held high, his line a gold thread in the sun, hanging in a graceful loop behind him. I motored slowly back toward the town. The car was a time machine, slipping like a breeze through the centuries, rolling past ancient stone houses and outbuildings and fields that had been tilled since before

Roman legions passed on their way to Spain or northern Gaul. And there was something more. As I passed slopes carpeted by olive groves, the thin leaves of the trees silvery grey against the sky, I realized what it was.

During the art gallery field trip when I had seen Ninon for the first time, with her jaunty beret and khaki greatcoat and clunky boots, I had learned that Van Gogh and other painters left northern Europe to paint in Provence. In Belgium and the Netherlands—and the place where I lived—the sun's rays struck the earth at an angle, reducing their intensity. Here, the sunlight poured down into the landscape and flooded the wheat fields and vineyards and fruit groves, illuminating every single blossom and stone and blade of grass, so that the world was bright and clear.

And on that day when I'd commented to Ninon that the sky in Van Gogh's painting of the yellow house couldn't have been that blue, she had said, "Oh, in Provence the sky is exactly like that."

And it was.

After lunch I left the hotel on foot, crossed the footbridge over the basin and followed the river a little way before turning into a lane barely wide enough to admit a car. Three- and four-storey shuttered stone buildings on each side formed a shaded canyon. I passed through Place de la Liberté, where a semicircle of shops, bakeries and a café faced the portals of a nine-hundred-year-old church. Plane trees shaded the cobblestones and the outdoor tables at the Café de France, where Ninon's father had once worked.

I pulled a map from my pocket. None of the lanes or alleys of this old original part of town followed a straight line—which made sense, in a way, since the village was encircled by the river and seamed by a network of clear shallow streams, some narrow enough to jump across, a few running right under the buildings. On the wider branches, huge iron water wheels at least four metres in diameter revolved slowly, their broad plank paddles and ancient frames green with moss, the water raining down from them in sheets. They had once powered small factories and mills. Now, disconnected, they rotated majestically on their axles with the flow of the Sorgue, like gears in a clock with no hands.

On the quai Frédéric Mistral I found the stone building where Ninon and her parents had lived and where her mother had kept her seamstress shop on the ground floor. The windows were covered by shutters painted yellow and blue. Downstream, within view of the windows, a water wheel revolved. I checked my watch against the position of the sun, then headed to my hotel.

I slept late the next morning. I had lots of time. When I came downstairs the patio tables on the river basin were already busy, the mid-morning sun bright and strong and sparkling on the water. I ate a couple of croissants, pulling them to bits with my fingertips, washing them down with café au lait, and watched the trout glide back and forth over the river's gravel bottom.

When the sun approached the right spot in the sky, I went to my room and pulled clothes from my backpack, replacing them with Ninon's funeral urn. I slung the pack onto my shoulders and headed into the village. Liberation Square lay striped and dappled with sunlight and the patio tables were full at the Café de France. I followed rue Pasteur to the quai Clovis Hughes, turned downstream, passing Ninon's home, and took the footbridge across the river. Along a short distance, a small landing allowed access to the water. A couple of ducks basked in the shade of the bank, heads tucked under their wings. I set down my backpack and took off my shoes. The ducks squawked their disapproval and plopped into the water and drifted downriver on the current.

I sat on the cement slab of the landing, swung my legs around and slipped into the icy river, sucking in my breath from the shock. I turned and removed the globe-shaped brass urn from the backpack and, clutching it tightly under one arm, felt my way along the gravel bottom, my free arm stretched wide for balance. The stones poked hard and cold under my stockinged feet, the relentless current dammed up against my legs.

I crept slowly into the flow, step by awkward step, my thighs quivering from the strain, until I was directly upstream from the water wheel. It revolved casually, its planks streaked with moss, the water hissing and showering like a million diamonds from the rising rust-coloured spokes and blades.

I heard a shout. Risked a glance toward the quay, where a small crowd had gathered. An old man in a jacket and necktie gesticulated with his cane. Others called out warnings, pointing at the water wheel. They wanted me to know that if I lost my balance and fell into the river I'd be swept under the wheel. But with the hot sun on my back, the fresh odour of the water in my nostrils, the aching cold on my skin, I held strong. And I felt a surge of happiness because I was able to do this last thing for the girl I loved. I had brought her home.

It was time. I braced my feet and legs and carefully unscrewed the top of the urn, dropping it into the river. Then, holding the urn firmly with both hands, I tipped it and gently shook Ninon's ashes into the Sorgue. Her dust ribboned away on the surface of the water, wavering and undulating as if alive, borne downriver to the turning wheel where one after another the broad blades caught her ashes and lifted them up, higher and higher, into the bluest of all the blue skies in the world.

ACKNOWLEDGMENTS

For generous sharing of their expertise, my sister, Carole Lashbrook, and Tony Gelmen; for reading the manuscript and offering ideas, my children, Dylan, Megan and Brendan Bell.

Thanks as always to my editor at Doubleday Canada, Amy Black, for her support, her insight and her patience.

And for everything, my soulmate, my first reader and helper, my inspiration and guide, Ting-xing Ye.